I0783632

Promise Keeper

PRAISE FOR
PROMISE KEEPER

A straightforward slow-burn queer love story with thoughtful
and frequent discussion of weighty topics.
-Kirkus Indie Reviews

Arzu depicts a nuanced protagonist whose journey mines
themes of colorism, class privilege, police brutality, and fraught
family dynamics. Chandon's convictions are admirable, and her
immersion into campus life is written with empathy, realism,
and the wonderment of emerging adulthood.
-Blue Ink Review

PROMISE KEEPER never loses sight of its values, nor of the
complexity and humanity of Black lives in America.
-Indie Reader

Also by Verde Arzu
Rainbow, a Black Queer Novella

Praise for
RAINBOW

An engaging work about the freedom that comes
with self-acceptance.
-Kirkus Indie Reviews

Verde Arzu's Rainbow is a touching, coming-of-age story
about learning to set aside other people's expectations and live
comfortably in your own sk**in.**
-Blue Ink Review

Verde Arzu's novella, RAINBOW, will easily draw in readers
of all backgrounds to experience a tale about Blackness, about
queerness, but also about one woman learning to allow all the
love that she deserves into her life.
-Indie Reader

⋆IR

Promise Keeper

A Novel

VERDE ARZU

RAINBOW EDITIONS | CALIFORNIA

An imprint of Rainbow Editions LLC, California

© 2025 Verde Arzu

All rights reserved under International and Pan-American Copyright Conventions. No portion of this book may be reproduced in any form or by any means, electronic or mechanical, including information storage and retrieval systems, without permission in writing from the publisher except by a reviewer, who may quote brief passages in review.

Published in the United States by Rainbow Editions, LLC 2025
Copyright © 2025 by Rainbow Editions, LLC
All rights reserved.
First Printing.

Promise Keeper is a work of fiction. Names, characters, places, and incidents are the product of the author's imagination or are used fictitiously. Any resemblance to actual persons, living or dead, events, or locales are entirely coincidental.

www.verdearzu.com
Cover Design & Interior Illustrations by E.A Wright.
(Chapters: 1, 8, 13 & 22)
Printed and bound in the United States of America.
ISBN: 979-8-9941332-1-7

I dedicate this book to Dashia, DaShaun, Rashad,
Trinity, Nyla, Elijah, Ariel, Isaiah, Marcus, and Thalia.
I think of you all in everything I do.

Remember to follow your dreams with reckless abandon.

Be so unbridled in your chase to achieve your dreams
that people look at you funny! ♥
-Love Always, TT Rae

And to mama, thank you for teaching me how to
write. I haven't stopped since.

And especially for *everything!*
-Baby Rae

"The things you do the most,
are the things you will do best."
-Marva N. Collins

Chapter One

I remembered the day I foolishly decided to use that old, unreliable elevator. No one was stupid enough to use the thing, at least not after their first week on campus. By then, everyone who lived in Giovanni Hall knew to steer clear of the some-timey elevator on the upper classmen side of our dorm building. But I had succumbed to hunger pains that were racking my belly, my dry throat longed to be quenched from the hours in the sticky, humid southern heat, and I felt cloaked with exhaustion from what seemed like miles of walking and chanting.

The collective voices of the people had risen and fallen like waves throughout the day, sometimes crashing in anger, other times retreating with exhaustion.

I knew it was a bad idea, but I stepped into the open elevator and hit the button anyway.

Just as the doors were closing shut, she slammed her arm between them. The doors quickly separated, and there she was. I couldn't stop staring at her overgrown jet-black Afro. It was tall in some places and poked out in others as if she had been lying on one side. Messy, but somehow accentuating her muscular jaw-line and defining her oval-shaped face.

Her white Chuck Taylors were gray from all the caked-on dirt, while the tattered shoestrings were barely tied. Her socks stopped just short of her runner's calves, and the uneven edges of her blue jean shorts looked homemade. The cut-off sleeves of her white t-shirt completed her look. She smiled back at me. I couldn't help but notice how her curly lashes accentuated the darkness of her round eyes, and they invited me in.

"Hey, Freshy, what are you doing? You haven't learned about this thing yet?" She licked her full brown lips and flashed another pearly white smile at me. "Well, let me tell you—"

"I know, I know," I said, sighing. "But I'm willing to take my chances right now."

"Well, your chances are pretty slim. Come on." She waved her hand and nodded her head, motioning me towards her. "You're gonna get stuck. And I would hate to have you on here all alone and scared." She flashed that charming smile at me again.

I sighed. "I've been on my feet for hours. I'm tired. I live on the seventh floor. The stairs are not an option today. Can you move out of the way so I can get to my room, please?" I said, slightly aggravated.

"Were you protesting or walking around the mall?"

"Yeah, I was."

"Yeah, you were what?" She folded her arms.

"Protesting," I shot back. "Were you?"

"Of course. I'm the president of the Black Student Union. Protesting is what I do," she said. Her chest seemed to protrude, and her shoulders straightened at that announcement.

"Come on, now. I heard one girl was stuck on here for a few hours." Her hand against the door prevented it from closing.

Two girls walked past. One in a white t-shirt with three blue Greek letters across the front, and the other in a blue tank with our school's name, Franklin, splayed across the top in golden block letters. They both had on flipflops and pajama pants and were carrying snacks and drinks.

"Let 'em learn, Corey!" Greek Blue Letters said.

"Yeah, they gotta learn," the other one added with a laugh. "Ol' captain save-a—"

Greek Letters shoved her friend's arm playfully, and they both continued down the hall, snickering and mumbling. Either Corey hadn't heard them, or she didn't care; she never even turned to acknowledge their presence.

She continued, "Well, since you have no intentions of getting off of this thing, I guess I'm going to have to ride with you."

She was inside before I could object, and the doors closed. I wasn't in a friendly, conversational mood. I had already walked more than I anticipated. All while screaming, yelling, singing, and demanding justice for yet another unarmed Black teen killed by police. My energy was drained, and I was rattled.

I stood in one corner of the elevator; she stood in the other. I stared at my blurry reflection in the scratched silver doors. My thick brown curly hair barely fit under my Chicago Cubs baseball cap, but I could make out the red "C". I focused my eyes there and waited.

"So, what did you think?" she asked.

"Think about what?" I asked, eyes still trained on the red "C".

"Think about the protest. We put that together—our BSU."

The protest flyers were posted all around campus. After class one day, as I stood reading one posted on the bulletin board, I overheard some of my classmates talking about it.

The video footage shows that he did steal from the store.

Yeah, so what? The cops didn't see the video footage. When does being accused of a crime justify taking your life? Isn't it 'innocent until proven guilty?' The other one asked as she stared back at her friend, waiting for an answer. There was a long pause.

Not for us. That don't apply to us.

Their conversation reminded me of the type of conversations my grandfather had with my grandmother, aunt, and uncle back home. He often made a similar 'that don't apply to us' argument when discussing the treatment Black people received from police officers.

And though I argued with my grandfather about the lack-luster outcomes marching and protesting had presently, my classmate's conversation made me feel like I had to do something. Travis Matthews was sixteen. Yes, the store's video surveillance showed he had taken the chips and soda from the neighborhood convenience store. Yes, he had run from the cops. But did it mean he deserved to be shot to death?

My mind drifted back to the metal cage I stood in. "Honestly, I went out there today hoping that it would change something because I was feeling helpless and hopeless," I said. "But on my walk back to campus, I was thinking that it's going to take more than some old-school marching to change things in the twenty-first century." I finally turned my head towards her.

"And what do you suggest we do?" she asked facetiously.

I sighed and looked at the light on the elevator, indicating the third floor. I wanted things to change, too, but standing in the heat chanting slogans felt like throwing pebbles at a mountain, hoping it would crumble.

The argument with Corey summoned my grandfather's stories about Franklin University, his words echoing in this elevator debate just as they had whenever I visited him. He was the reason I had chosen Franklin. He bragged so much about his precious alma mater, Franklin University, a historically Black university.

He was always telling me stories about his and my grandmother's time here. How they met and fell in love during a Student Nonviolent Coordinating Committee meeting. They had both been active in civil rights protests, demonstrations, and sit-ins.

I wanted to make him proud of me. I wanted to show him that I wasn't afraid or ashamed of my Blackness, though he might think I was.

Mainly, I was tired of silently listening to him lecture me about what I didn't know and how it was my mother's fault I didn't know these things because *'yo' daddy decided to marry a White woman.'* And the truth? He would've been right there with Corey, chanting in step. And here I was, still questioning if any of it mattered.

"Well, what are your ideas? What are *you* doing?" Corey kept tapping her foot.

I could feel the rumbling vibration of the elevator underneath my own feet. I clutched the cold, hard rail as we continued to move.

"Listen, I'm not knocking your efforts today. Not at all. It was good and necessary. But Black people have been marching and protesting for fifty-plus years, is all I'm saying, and what have we got?"

"Uh, does the Civil Rights Act of '64 and the Voting Rights Act of '65 ring a bell to you at all? Come on! All that marching and protesting moved this country forward." She seemed annoyed.

"Yet here we are," I said, shrugging.

"Oh my God!" she groaned. But before she could say anything more, the lights flickered, and the chains on the elevators screeched and squealed like a speeding locomotive train slamming its brakes. The elevator rattled like a California earthquake.

The metal cage shuddered around us, the air suddenly thick with the scent of hot metal and dust. Our bodies jerked with its movement. One of my hands squeezed the hard rail tighter while the other reached for my dad's dog tags that always hung around my neck. The number five on the elevator panel lit up and then flickered out. The sound of the motor was no more. We were stopped right before the sixth floor.

"Fuck!" I said and kicked the elevator's wall.

"Stay calm," she said and hit the red emergency button. "The thing is, it's going to take someone *at least* thirty minutes to respond. So, get comfortable. You stubborn know-it-all freshmen." She shook her head and slid down to sit on the floor.

"I didn't tell you to get on here with me. I was fine by myself," I replied. I bit my thumb nail as I stared at her scrunched up on the floor, knees tucked to her chest.

"Right. Would you rather be in this position right now alone…or with me?" She flashed that smile of hers again. "Don't answer that. I already know."

I walked over and hit the red emergency button again.

"Ain't gon' help. They're going to respond when they respond."

"What is *that* supposed to mean? This button is here for *emergencies.*"

"Same reason we march. We press the button and alert the people that there is an emergency. The response won't always be fast, but there will be a response. So, sit down and wait. Or you can keep kicking the walls on this piece of shit, and we can both fall to our deaths."

"Wow! Bravo!" I clapped sarcastically. "You must be a speech major."

"Nope. History," she smirked. "And thank you."

I rolled my eyes. Her analogy was well-crafted, but I wasn't ready to concede my point.

"We need to be more aggressive…The Black Panther Party and Malcolm X had the right ideas. We have to protect ourselves! We have to police our communities," I said, my fingers unconsciously tightening around the elevator rail.

"Oh, you believe in segregation," she said in a baffled tone.

"No," I sighed. They believed in the uplifting of their people.

My head and feet hurt. I had walked and walked all day in the sweltering heat—and, at the end of it, I was still feeling helpless and hopeless. Travis Matthew, the young man we were marching for, was still dead. Still killed by the cops who had sworn to protect him.

"You got a lot of words and opinions but no real, concrete ideas, strategies, and plans for us to use. At least when we're marching in the streets, we're moving, and our voices are being heard.

"We're out there letting the community know we're with them, we're together, and we are one. When one of us is hurt or killed, it affects us all. Marching is just one facet—the quickest and most visible response. The government killed Malcolm and destroyed the Panthers. We must learn from that, too," she said passionately.

"Yeah, *and* Martin…and he was non-violent." I added.

"You know, it's people like you who really discourage me. You're all about criticizing what we're doing, but you ain't joining no movements. You're not even a member of your school's BSU! That should've been your first campus meeting, Freshy." She rolled her eyes and put her head in her hands. "I should've let you take this ride to nowhere alone."

"Yeah, because you're so comforting right now."

"Listen, Freshy, there'll be plenty of time for hugging and kissing, but first, you gotta be woke up."

"Woke up or thinking exactly like you?"

"I can't fuck with nobody who ain't woke."

"Fuck with? *Me?* I don't think so. That's pretty presumptuous of you, don't you think?" I didn't know who this girl thought she was, or who the hell she thought *I* was, but interested in her, I was not.

She jumped up and dusted off her butt with her hands, then walked calmly over to me. She stood directly in front of me.

"Freshy, trust me. If I wanted there to be hugs and kisses, that's what there would be right now. I wouldn't have gotten on this piece of shit asking you about no protest or marching if that's what I was on. You understand?" I watched the muscles in her jaws clench.

I could feel her warm breath against my skin. Her gaze, deep and unwavering, held mine. Her round eyes gleamed with a quiet intensity. There was a power in her presence, subtle yet undeniable as if the very air around us hummed with her energy. Her words carried the weight of certainty, each one landing like a professor's lecture rather than a student's opinion.

My chest tightened and moved as if I had jogged to where I stood. I tried to control it, but I couldn't. A shiver raced through my body. I grabbed my arms where the goosebumps prickled my skin, trying to rub them away and calm my nerves. I took a step back from her imposing frame, but the warm sensation remained. Its vibration danced and rushed through me, settling in between my thighs. *She's arrogant, rude, demanding, annoying—so annoying! I mean, who does she think she is? And strong.* Yes, strong. God. I'd never met anyone like her.

My back pressed into the cool elevator's walls while my arms reached along its railings, my hands firmly gripping them. I crossed one leg over the other and tried to play it cool while I gave her another once-over. She was a little bit taller than my five-six frame, though the Afro made her appear much taller. I took in her tattered shirt again, her flexed arms showing her muscles, her hair wild and free. *That hair suits you,* I thought. Her skin was a chocolate drop, Hershey's Kiss smooth brown. But those glasses with the tape around one of the arms—ridiculous!

Just get them fixed! Ugh! Who does she think she is, talking with all this audacity and authority?

I was caught off-guard. But I was in no way about to back down.

"My name is Chandon, not Freshy," I managed. I slid over to the corner away from her. I could feel my heart starting to race. I twirled the rainbow wristlet Asher had given me this summer, the colors blurring together as my thoughts spun back to Stephanie.

Asher didn't want me to keep the closed-off mentality I had in high school after my girlfriend, Stephanie, and I were torn apart.

My mind traveled back to Stephanie. Her blazing, straight red hair matched her fiery personality, a splash of that demanding attention against her smooth ivory skin. Her hazel green eyes melted my heart every time she smiled back at me. The most beautiful girl I knew. Smart. Independent. Fun.

Her mother thought we were just friends, until the day we cut school. Stephanie said she'd be out of town, but she came home early.

When she walked into Stephanie's room, there was nothing left to be said. We'd fallen asleep in each other arms…naked. Stephanie was sent off to some boarding school far away, where they still secretly offered conversion therapy. I got one single letter from her six months after she was stolen from me. In it, she told me she was okay. That she realized what we had been doing was "sinful and overstepped our friendship." The letter crushed me to my core. I spent a week in bed, lying to my mother about being sick. It had been two years since that letter.

"Oh, I know what your name is," Corey said, jolting me out of my thoughts. "Chandon Kilpatrick." The way my name rolled off her tongue sent an unexpected shiver down my spine. She leaned her shoulder against the wall and folded her arms.

Whiffs of her cocoa butter scent invited me in. I hadn't felt the butterflies that fluttered in my stomach since Stephanie. Thinking of her made me miss home but also brought back that terrible knot of fear. The way Stephanie had been torn from me, how we'd been punished for our feelings. Now here I was, trapped in this elevator, those same forbidden butterflies taking flight.

My chest tightened as conflicting emotions collided. The attraction. The fear of where it might lead. The memory of loss. I began to breathe heavier like I was gasping for air. The small space seemed to shrink further, the walls closing in with each passing second.

My lungs burned with each shallow breath, my shirt suddenly clinging to my damp skin, the elevator walls seeming to pulse inward with each frantic heartbeat. I felt a sweaty, warm rush from my head down to my feet. Was I having a heart attack? I placed my hand over my pounding heart. The space of the elevator seemed tighter and more confining than before.

"I—I—I can't breathe. Oh, God, I can't breathe," I panted. "I need air! I need air!"

Corey's eyes widened with alarm. She stepped toward me cautiously, her earlier confidence replaced with genuine concern.

"Hey, hey, calm down. Relax, shh, shh," Corey rushed to me and rubbed my arms. "Breathe in, slow and steady, through your nose and out through your mouth. Look at me, look at me. You're all right, okay? Someone is coming. Just stay calm and relax. You're not having a heart attack. Okay? Keep breathing. Here, sit down." Corey helped me to the floor and sat next to me.

"Take your shirt off," she instructed.

My eyes widened.

"Trust me. It'll help. I'm not trying to—just take your shirt off."

I reluctantly pulled my shirt over my head. I was more aware and concerned with my A-cup breasts than I wanted to admit. She took my shirt from me and wiped my forehead, neck, shoulders, and back. Then she waved it in front of me like a fan.

"Just think about something that'll calm you down…we're on the beach. It's a warm day. The sun is beaming down. The waves are crashing. Can you hear them? We're reclined in beach chairs, debating whether we're going to go jump into the ocean. You hear those birds singing? They're singing your favorite song. Damn, don't you just love and envy birds?" Her voice was calm and low.

The elevator jolted hard. Its engine rumbled and started, and then the metal cage began to move again.

"We've got you moving!" A woman's staticky voice blurted through the emergency intercom.

I saw the number six light up and go out, then the number seven. I closed my eyes and prayed to hear the ding of the elevator doors opening. Corey rushed to the door and held it open with her arm. I pulled my shirt back over my head.

"Come on, let's get you off of this thing," she said, her voice still calm and soothing.

As I stepped out, she reached out to rub my arm reassuringly.

"You okay, Freshy?"

I jerked my arm away from her touch. "Chandon, my name is Chandon."

"Right. Okay. Well, see you later, then," she said and turned and walked away.

My words were jammed up in my throat, unwilling to crack my stubborn lips. I just stood there and watched her walk off.

Chapter Two

After the elevator incident, I found myself thinking about Stephanie and decided to join All Colors United, the LGBTQ+ group on campus. It was a huge step for me. Joining this club could be a chance for me to do something with all of the hurt, pain, and emotions besides block them out of my heart and mind like she had never happened. The fact of the matter was that no matter how much I tried to forget her, I thought about Stephanie almost every day.

My grandfather called asking me which clubs I was involved in. I lied and told him I hadn't done any of that yet. Without hesitation and on cue, he told me I needed to 'get involved' on campus.

"A marriage is between a man and a woman, Daniel. Period," I recalled him telling my uncle Dee one day while they both stood in the backyard at the barbecue grill talking and drinking. So, I knew being a member of ACU would not have made him proud. Instead, I would have been bombarded with questions. I wasn't ready for that. My mom and aunt Ronda knew who I was and that was good enough for me.

At the first meet and greet for ACU, one person stood out. Her name was Alisha; we were in math class together but hadn't spoken to each other before. She was cute and friendly, I thought to myself.

The ACU meetings took place in one of the homes turned office spaces on campus. This house was called *Hester House*. The meeting was the first time I had ever heard of Rita Hester. I learned that she was a Black transgender woman who had been murdered—stabbed to death in her own home. This was shortly after Matthew Shepard's gruesome murder. Both murders were deemed hate crimes.

Unlike Shepard's, though, her murder and life garnered little media coverage or visibility, and it was never solved. Rita was known as a vibrant, active woman in her community who lived out loud and unashamed.

"We are marginalized, murdered, and left to suffer in silence and anguish," the ACU President, Chris Ford, said that day as he stood before us in the living room of Hester House. "But together, we say, no more! Our lives matter, our stories matter, and we will not remain silent." He rallied to the applause of current members who echoed back bold shouts of "No more!", their fists raised high into the air. I could feel the blood rushing through my body as my heart thumped.

I listened to our ACU president talk about Rita Hester and describe her as a bold leader. With every word he spoke, there was an electricity that moved around the room, a collective buzz that moved through my veins. I closed my eyes and let the determined voices around me intertwine and pulse with the blood rushing through me. The moment exhilarated me in a way that I had never felt before. When I opened my eyes, I realized I wasn't just listening to the speech—I was becoming a part of it. It was liberating.

I learned so much history in that first meeting. As Chris continued speaking, he transported us back to 2006, when Franklin's LGBTQ+ students had banded together, protested and demanded space on our traditionally Christian, conservative campus. Their activism had been sparked by tragedy—the suicide of sophomore student C.J. Malcolm.

She was a transgender student who committed suicide after being bullied and isolated. I was inspired by our president, Chris, who stood before us with so much confidence and poise. He spoke with so much passion, recommitting to ACU's mission that no other student would ever suffer C.J.'s experience.

Chris shared C.J.'s devastating story. One fall evening, as she was leaving the library, C.J. was beaten and robbed at gunpoint and left for dead, unconscious on the sidewalk. Not one single witness. Rumors spread like wildfire. The attackers were outsiders. They were paid on a dare. Worse, some thought she'd gotten what she deserved.

Weeks after the horrific attack, C.J. left behind a detailed note describing her experiences on campus, recounting the relentless torment she faced daily. In it, she wrote about the isolation that engulfed her, about how she was treated like an outsider, an invisible presence—someone whose pain didn't matter. Like she didn't matter, she wasn't human, she was "other".

The room fell silent as Chris's words hung in the air. In that heavy moment, my thoughts inevitably drifted to Stephanie. Her smile, red hair, smooth skin, and hazel green eyes played across the movie screen of my mind. My heart sank to my stomach. How was she doing after "boarding school?" Had she made it to college somewhere? Was she still carrying the wounds of isolation like C.J. had?

The parallels between C.J.'s story and what Stephanie had endured just a couple of years ago were impossible to ignore. A lump swelled in my throat, and I quickly shook the thought away, forcing myself to refocus on Chris's account of ACU's history.

"After months of protesting," Chris continued, his voice growing stronger, "even with threats of expulsion from the administration, those students refused to stop."

They wanted Franklin University's anti-gay student code of conduct changed. The policy barred students from forming groups related to their identity or sexual orientation. They could not access school funds set aside by the university to support clubs and student-lead organizations because it would go "against scripture." These rules created a culture of hate and isolation for C.J. Malcolm, the students argued.

The protests began to gather city, state, and eventually national attention. Support from other campus clubs and organizations surged as well. After several months, the executive board and campus leadership responded and allowed the students to occupy a classroom that eventually evolved into a permanent house on campus. ACU named the house in honor of Rita Hester "to ensure hers and others' lives would be remembered."

"Ultimately," Chris said, lowering his voice to emphasize the victory, "the student code of conduct was revised to 'welcome all students with love, following in the footsteps of Christ and Christian values'."

The room seemed to exhale collectively. Chris scanned the faces of everyone present before his gaze settled on mine. I felt as if he was looking directly into my eyes when he said, "You are not here by accident."

He reminded us that we stood on the shoulders of Rita Hester, Matthew Shepard, C.J. Malcolm, and so many others, their lives were the ultimate sacrifice. Their names hung heavy in the air, pressing down on us like a weight we were meant to carry forward.

I wiped away the tears that escaped from my watery eyes as I shook my head and accepted his words. I knew then that ACU was where I belonged.

Hester House itself seemed to embrace us as we sat there. Many of its original finishes had been preserved during renovation. Like the oak wood floors that creaked and groaned with every step, and silver cast iron radiators lining the walls. Two three-seater brown leather chesterfield couches rested in front of each other, a dark mahogany wood coffee table with cabriole legs at their center.

The couches were surrounded by wingback chairs with a variety of faded, discolored seats. I was sitting in one of the old side chairs that made you sink deeper and lower than you expected or wanted. These chairs were flanked by armchairs with seat backs as worn-out as the seat cushions and arms. Floor-to-ceiling bookshelves lined the walls in every room. Some books were so old the scent of their musty pages wafted into the space; they made me feel even more cozy and welcomed.

The ACU meeting spoke to me and moved me like no experience I had before. Sitting in that historic space, surrounded by both current students and echoes of the past, a memory surfaced—my grandfather's weathered voice describing his time at Franklin as a member of the Black Student Union.

"Sometimes finding your people is what gives you the strength to make change," he'd told me once.

For the first time, I truly understood what he meant. I was settled: I would tell him about ACU. It was my decision to make, not his.

In the next few weeks, after officially joining ACU, I began to learn about the various committees I could join. One of them was called *Loud & Proud at School*, a fundraising group for high school and middle school students, which I loved right away.

The money the *Loud & Proud* committee fundraised went towards anti-bullying and prevention programs, supporting activities at schools, providing funding for field trips, personal supplies, and assistance with helping schools start up their clubs and safe spaces for LGBTQ+ youth.

I thought this committee was amazing. My fingers traced the glossy fundraising pamphlet as I imagined how different things might have been just a year ago. This was exactly the support I needed when I was in high school—someone to tell me it gets better.

The memory of my sophomore year came rushing back: the silence in the hallways after Stephanie was taken away, the way I'd folded into myself, building walls no one could breach. Maybe with a group like this, I wouldn't have shut down and isolated myself so completely.

For as long as I could remember, I was attracted to girls, that wasn't a big deal for me to accept. The problem was dealing with people who had a problem with it. Especially my grandfather, because I only wanted to make him proud of me.

Demand to be Safe & Gay was the other committee I looked at closely. It focused on bringing awareness to LGBTQ+ crisis situations. Like the two USA military veterans who were imprisoned in Kuwait. Monica Jacobs and Lorraine Cuttleston claimed their arrest and detention wasn't about possession of illegal drugs. They argued they were targeted for being gay in a country that criminalized same-sex relationships.

Both Monica and Lorraine had served seven years in the United States Army and remained in Kuwait to work as military contractors. I felt my heart sink to my stomach when I first learned their story. The cool metal of the dog tags I always wore pressed against my chest suddenly felt heavier. I found myself clutching them in the palm of my hand, the familiar ridges of the embossed letters connecting me instantly to my dad. As the present moment blurred, all I could see was his uniform photo on our mantel at home.

I don't remember much about him, just flashes. The way his arms looked when he held me. The deep sound of his voice rumbling under my cheek. I was only four when he died, but that photo? It's burned into my mind like a memory I chose to keep repeating, even when the others faded. I didn't have the words for it back then, but maybe that was the first promise I ever made—to make his sacrifice mean something.

After he finished his service, my dad also worked as a military contractor. He had returned home for a few years as a civilian but wanted to buy a house for his family. He would make more than double the amount as a military contract worker than if he stayed stateside for work.

It would only be for a year, he said. Just enough time to save a substantial amount of money for the down payment. It was dangerous, but my dad would be extra safe. He promised my mom. So, she reluctantly agreed.

My mom said she wanted to protect my brother and me from the details of what happened to our dad. But after I turned sixteen, I demanded to know.

That afternoon remains crystallized in my memory. Mom sat me down at our kitchen table, her pale hands trembling slightly as she told me everything she knew. The convoy my dad drove with was headed back to their base when a suicide bomber, driving a car packed full of what looked like a large family, children included, detonated on the road directly in front of them. Before any of the soldiers could react, the car exploded. There were no survivors in my dad's military vehicle.

The aftermath of his death had only deepened the rift between my mother and grandfather. A divide that had existed since the day my parents announced their engagement. My grandfather, who had never approved of his son marrying a White woman, had a target for all his grief and anger.

Years later, I could still hear his voice booming through his house after he'd had a few drinks: "She had no business telling him to go back over there! Greedy-ass White woman! Ain't no Black woman letting her husband stay in no damn war zone after she done married him and had two kids by him. Only white people crazy enough to do that! I told his ass not to marry her. He finished his service, dammit! He should've been home!"

"Now, that's enough, Emanuel," my grandmother would warn him whenever she saw me or my brother listening to one of these rants.

"The man had a G.I Bill, Myra. That wasn't enough, huh? She needed more," he'd go on anyway.

"You raised E.J. to be a man and make his own choices, now. He was trying to provide for his family the best way *he* knew how. The Lord has his reasons. Elizabeth is not to blame, and you know that. She's raising his babies up as best she can."

My grandmother tried to comfort him with a light touch of her hand on his or the kind of hug only she could give. But when he went on one of his rants, there was no stopping him, especially after several brown colored drinks or if any of my uncles were around drinking with him in the kitchen or his study, which had books stacked from floor to ceiling on its shelves.

My grandma would cradle or hug my brother and me and tell us he didn't mean it; he was just hurting from missing his youngest son. His 'baby boy'. She'd usher us into the kitchen and sit us at the counter or table for cake, pie, or ice cream. But none of it ever made me feel any better.

My mother would never put anyone she loved in harm's way, I thought. How could my grandfather say those things even if he was hurting? She wasn't the Taliban; she was his wife. White or not, she was his wife, and she loved him. I knew this.

The way my mom would talk about him made a part of me—the part of me that imagined he was still here—feel like I knew him better than I really did. She made sure we knew he loved us and wanted the best for us.

I knew *Demand to be Safe & Gay* was the committee I had to join. I'd do it in my father's honor. He would've wanted me to fight to help bring those two U.S. veterans back home.

He'd be proud of me. That much I knew for sure.

Chapter Three

Although it had been a few weeks since I'd seen her, Corey's voice remained in the back of my mind like an echo that refused to fade. I knew I wasn't going to be a member of the Black Student Union, but that didn't mean I couldn't check them out and see what was going on. I just hadn't yet found the right time. At least, that's what I told myself.

I thought about how being a member of BSU would ease the tension in the conversation I would have with my grandfather about joining ACU. Then, I realized I would still be doing what *he* wanted me to do.

However, I also had to be honest with myself about the fear I felt about joining BSU. According to my grandfather, I wasn't Black enough. At least, he always made me feel that way. Attending Franklin was supposed to show him that wasn't true. Yet, inside of myself, I still questioned whether my light skin *was* Black enough.

I certainly didn't feel White enough. In high school, although I was never called out by my name or experienced any of the things my grandparents, aunt, and uncle talked about, there was never a time when I didn't stand out amongst my friends, didn't feel there was something different about me. I felt caught somewhere in the in-between. Not enough. I really didn't have anyone in my family who I could talk to about it either. I just kept trying to fit in wherever I was.

ACU didn't make me feel like that. I wanted to explain all of this to Corey. But how could I? Would she be able to understand me if I did? Would I be able to trust that she would try to understand me?

After class one late afternoon, I walked the sidewalk along the sprawling, immaculately cut green grass, accentuated by the reddish cobblestone roads and surrounded by the tall historic, early twentieth century brick buildings. They stood like well-dressed, sophisticated people from high society, ready to serve students tea, crumpets, and a high-quality education.

The meticulously cut bushes surrounding each building, with well-fertilized flowers in bloom, the colors of Crayola, danced along the entry paths. Each spring, the campus brought its fair share of tourists to its historically protected hills.

I passed the Malcolm X & Betty Shabazz Library and stared at the gothic-style brick DuBois Hall. It demanded everyone's attention, standing tall as if dressed in a ball gown, regal and commanding. At its center, the Roman numeral clock sat pinned like a brooch, chiming every hour, marking time with unwavering precision.

In the middle of the lawn, a bronze, timeworn statue of W.E.B. DuBois stood bold and resolute. The short, stout man rested atop a square stone block, a stack of books clutched in his grasp, an homage to his life's work as an American sociologist, civil rights activist, and icon.

DuBois attended Fisk University, another historically Black college. He was the first Black American to earn a PhD from Harvard. DuBois symbolized the epitome of Black power and excellence—because if he could do it, so could we. It was our daily, undeniable visual reminder.

Then, right smack dab at the front of the campus, like a majestic castle, stood the university's centerpiece. The historic Nash-Jamison Hall. Its Gothic Revival architecture echoing the grandeur of seventeenth-century England.

Erected in the late nineteenth century by architect John Lewis, the tower carried the weight of history in its stone and intricate spires. The bell housed within once served as an alarm system, warning past students of impending racist attacks from the American terrorist organization, the Ku Klux Klan.

Now, it stood not as a warning but a beacon of resilience, home to community and campus social and political events, along with freshmen morning and afternoon classes.

During the day, the strikingly tall building shone with pride, surrounded by the tallest, greenest pine trees, which gave more of an aura of protective sentinels than cool shade. At night, the bell tower glowed with a warm mystique, its light casting long shadows that stretched across the campus like whispers from the past. Walking along the circular paved path up to the building, I could feel its magic, mystery, and the spiritual pull of its energy.

It was a historic monument built with brick, not for aesthetics' sake, but as a barrier against intentional fires meant to burn it to rubble and ashes. The grounds felt as hallowed as my grandfather described during his many rambling trips down memory lane.

I continued walking up the path, my eyes fixed on the sun sinking behind Nash-Jamison Hall, its golden light casting a final glow over the towering structure. The bell tower began to glow, flickering to life like an ember catching breath.

I was just turning left along the path, heading toward my dorm room, when her voice snapped me out of my thoughts, quick and unexpected like someone tapping me on my shoulder when I wasn't looking.

"You not coming?" Her voice startled me.

"Coming where?" I turned around to see Alisha smiling back at me.

"You haven't heard? BSU is hosting our city's Black Lives Matter chapter here in N.J. Hall tonight. They're here because they want to hear from us, the students, before their next town hall meeting. I'm so excited!" She bit her bottom lip and gave a fist pump.

Alisha was a freshman like me. I noticed how she was always smiling, filled with positivity, bubbly, and didn't shy away from talking. I'd already noticed her at the first ACU meeting; she'd walked right up and introduced herself.

We'd hit it off because my "mm-hmms" and "yeahs" were just enough to keep the conversation going. Her thick curves, bright smile, and freckled nose and cheeks were easy on the eyes, too. I found it effortless, listening to her run-on sentences.

"So, I know you coming, right?" she stood with her hand on her hip, waiting. As soon as I opened my mouth to speak, she grabbed my arm. "Girl, come on!"

She pulled me back onto the path up to the shining building. For me, going inside the six-story Victorian-Gothic style Nash-Jamison Hall was like walking into a sacred cathedral. The first thing anyone saw when they walked in was a sprawling wooden staircase with hand-carved banister rails that seemed to lead up to heaven. Antique chandeliers hung from the ceiling, their crystals catching the light like scattered diamonds.

The well-polished parquet floors gleamed beneath them, reflecting years of footsteps, conversations, and untold history. I could *feel* the presence of the many years of historical moments the building preserved. The pearl-white walls held secrets between their wainscoting and crown molding, whispering silent stories only they would ever know.

The curtains that hung from the huge floor-to-ceiling windows were opulent, a deep royal blue with gold trim. They draped like heavy robes, regal and commanding; beneath them, several layers of luxurious, textured fabric cascaded down like extravagant silk nightgowns, delicate yet deliberate in their elegance. The meeting took place in the ballroom called Queen Ella, named after one of the school's founders.

Upon entering, a gigantic, floor-to-ceiling, vibrantly colored painting of the eleven founders of Franklin University on the front wall commanded attention. Dressed in the finest clothing of the late 1800s, they gazed out with an air of quiet dignity, their presence almost alive in the strokes of the artist's brush.

Folks came from all over the world to tour the hand-painted image, admiring the richness of its detail and the weight of history it carried. As I stood in the space, the leaders of the city's Black Lives Matter chapter stood in front of the painting, where they addressed a large crowd—mostly students.

The hum of the crowd's voices softened as BLM leaders began to speak, their energy filling the room as naturally as the light filtering in through the grand windows. I listened carefully as they discussed their ten-point program, each word landing like a steady drumbeat, grounding me in the moment.

"We are clear about our demands for police accountability. Police officers must be required to wear body cameras during any stop! Dashboard cameras should be installed in every vehicle. It is our tax dollars that are paying the families of our slain sisters and brothers while the murderers continue to hide behind their badges." The short but powerful-voiced woman spoke as she stood behind the lectern.

She gripped the microphone tightly in her hand, her fingers wrapped around it like a lifeline. As she scanned the crowd, her eyebrows pulled close together, and her lips pressed into a firm line.

"But these murders are already being caught on camera, so what difference will that make?"

A student called out from the crowd. Their voice, slicing through the air, met with murmurs of agreement.

"These body cameras and dash cameras will be required equipment, like carrying their gun or taser. The evidence will come directly from the source. No excuses," she responded confidently.

"I'll leave you all with the words of our revolutionary leader Assata Shakur: 'It is our duty to fight for our freedom. It is our duty to win. We must love each other and support each other. We have nothing to lose but our chains.' Free Assata Shakur! Free all political prisoners!" she roared, her voice swelling as she closed the discussion and stepped away from the podium.

Fists flew into the air, some still, some unmoving, others pumping in rhythm of the growing chants of "Black Lives Matter."

People surged toward the podium, swarming around her and the three other speakers like fans rushing a superstar at a free concert with no security. I lingered for a moment, watching the crowd's enthusiastic response, then quietly slipped away from the packed room. The energy had been overwhelming—exactly what I needed, but also exhausting.

As I stepped outside into the evening air, I took a deep breath, letting the cooler temperature clear my head. I walked across the yard, heading back to my dorm room, my eyes scanning the large groups of students moving in every direction around me.

The meeting had drawn a huge turnout, and everywhere, voices buzzed with chatter, loud discussions rippling through the crowd. The air was charged, thick with passion, excitement, and the electricity of new ideas. I was glad to be walking back alone. I needed to think.

"Yo, Freshy! Wait up," I heard a voice call behind me. I recognized it right away. A twirl of excitement danced in my stomach, light and sudden, like a leaf caught in a gust of wind. *Ugh! Play it cool*, I scolded myself. I turned around, filled with excitement, though I tried not to show it.

"Corey, right?" I said as if I had forgotten.

She paused, eyes sweeping over me, looking me up and down like she didn't believe me. "Yeah…right."

"I'd really prefer it if you would just call me by my name."

"My bad. Freshy just kinda flows with you, you know? It's just that you're so cute."

I tensed at her compliment, warmth creeping up my neck before I could stop it.

"Just don't get mad at me if it slips out," she continued.

"And don't get mad at me if I correct you. The last time, you walked off like *you* were offended."

"The last time you acted like I had cooties as soon as we were off the elevator and in public. I didn't appreciate that shit."

My head and eyes lowered to the ground instantly, heat creeping further up my face. The weight of her words settled heavily in my chest.

"Yeah, I know. I'm sorry about that." I said it sincerely, my voice quieter, softer.

"It's all good. Just don't let it happen again," she said.

She gave me that bright, mischievous smile, bit her bottom lip, and surveyed my body from head to toe. Her gaze lingered, slow and deliberate, like she was studying something worth remembering. I wondered how many other girls on campus she gave that look to. I started to walk.

"Anyway, you're not one of those closeted homos, are you?"

I stopped mid-stride, the question hitting me like a sudden gust of wind.

"Wow!" I shook my head in disbelief, a dry laugh escaping before I could stop it.

"Well, if I wasn't out, I would be now."

She looked around, her gaze sweeping the space as if checking for eavesdroppers.

"You right. You right. My bad, my bad," she said, patting her chest in quick succession, the sound light but certain—like knocking on a door she already knew would open. "But it's two-thousand and fifteen! Fuck what people think."

We stood, glancing at each other, the air between us thick with something unspoken. She broke our silence with a burst of excitement, her energy cracking through the stillness like a sudden spark.

"Hey, I see you went to the Black Lives Matter meeting tonight! Just say the word, and I'll make sure there's a seat for you next to me in the car I'll be riding in to go to the protest next week." She smiled, those long, bright, shiny teeth framed by her thick, plump brown lips.

This time I blushed, holding back my smile as best I could. I started walking again. "I don't know. I need to check and see what's happening with ACU and what we're—"

"ACU?!" she interjected.

"Yeah, I—" My words caught in my throat as her tone changed.

"You joined ACU over BSU? What? Why?"

"What do you mean 'over'?" I felt my chest tighten.

"*Over*, meaning ahead of or before. You haven't joined BSU yet. What's up with that? I've been waiting to see you show up." Her eyes fixed on mine, expectant.

I paused. She had been waiting on me. The thought created a stir in my stomach like the glow of a low-burning ember.

"Actually, I don't know if I'm going to join BSU," I responded.

Her bright smile was gone. Her face became a scowl. "While Black and Brown men and women are killed every day by the police?!"

"It doesn't need to make sense to *you*; it's *my* decision. It only has to make sense to me." I began taking faster strides, my heart pounding against my ribs. This wasn't just about a club choice—it was about who got to define me—to decide for me, what I should do.

"When you walk down the street, the first thing the police see—hell, *everyone* sees—is a Black woman. Not a—a lesbian. You're automatically profiled by the color of your skin! That's not your fight?"

"Hate crimes and violence against openly gay people happen all the time! Our transgender women are being murdered for sport! Just for what they wear and how they look.

"And what about the seven Black women in New York? They were walking down the street at night, minding their own business, and were attacked for being gay. They were called "The Gang of Killer Lesbians' by the media."

My voice caught as I added, "When I first read about them, I couldn't sleep for days. Are you going to say that sexuality, gender, has nothing to do with that?"

"Of course it does," Corey conceded, then pulled my arm and stopped me from walking. At the touch of her hand, I felt a tingling sensation rush through me and land in the middle of my thighs, but I wasn't going to allow that feeling to stop me from proving my point.

"You just finished asking me if I were 'out' as if it's totally unacceptable *not* to be." My voice was raised and breaking. "Well, some people can't be out for fear of their safety—in 2015, no less! And, if you can't see that, then you're delusional!" I was trembling, my hands making sharp gestures I couldn't control. "Angela Davis once said, 'You either assent to homophobia or you speak out against it!'"

The quote came out more rehearsed than I intended like I was arguing with my grandfather or arguing a point in class. This wasn't a classroom debate. This was my life. But the truth behind those words still burned in me.

"Hold up, Dre." I saw one of the students passing by pull on his friend's t-shirt. They changed direction and walked over towards us. That's when I noticed a small crowd beginning to gather around us. Their eyes were wide; some stood with their arms folded, holding their backpack straps or leaning into each other, whispering a statement either I or Corey had made.

The air felt suddenly thicker, charged with expectation. I took a deep breath and looked back toward Corey.

"But those are just clothes, not the color of someone's skin, Chandon."

She had finally said my name. I was stuck there momentarily, listening to the sound of my name roll off her lips. The sound played over in my head like a scratched CD in an endless loop. I shook myself out of my trance and urged myself to stay focused.

Her dismissal of clothing as "just clothes" struck a nerve. I thought about Stephanie. *My* Stephanie, who sneaked clothes out of her older brother's closet and changed into them in the girl's bathroom each morning she arrived at school. She said the ruffled shoulder polyester shirts with colorful fruits and flowers, the skirts and dresses her mother continued to buy, despite her objections, made her feel imprisoned like she was being stitched into a version of herself that wasn't real. The fabric scratched against her skin as a constant reminder of the lie she was forced to portray to make her mother happy.

"And why aren't you a member of ACU? We're trying to change things, too. And not just for one specific group."

"One specific group? That's what you think? BSU is for the people, all groups of oppressed people. Black Lives Matter is against police brutality and the oppression of people in America and around the world, period. Specifically, against that of Black people, hence the word Black, but there wouldn't be a need for a Black anything if we weren't being gunned down at the rate of more than one thousand Black lives a year in this country!"

I heard some "mm-hmms," and "yeah, that's truth." A few people even clapped, the sound sharp and deliberate, punctuating the air like exclamation points. I had found myself in the middle of a debate, and I wasn't going to back down from it.

"'Hence the word *Black*', yeah, and that's what excludes *all* groups of people right there."

"Well, if *all* people were being gunned down by police at such an alarming rate the organization would be called something else. If you're caught up on the word *Black,* then you're confused and a part of the problem."

People were hooting, clapping, and pumping their fists in the air in support of Corey.

"She must think she ain't Black," I heard someone yell from the back of the crowd, which produced a chuckle from many of those surrounding us.

I felt my heart drop to my stomach. The callous dismissal of my identity hit harder than any argument Corey made. My grandfather's voice echoed in my head. His comments about my mother, his expectations of how I should identify, who I should be. I was afraid to look into the crowd. It wasn't just about losing this argument; it was about being rejected by a community—a community that was a part of me.

"You can't see how saying *Black Lives Matter* might make some people feel excluded? You can't understand where I'm coming from at all?" I pleaded.

"Some people? You mean *you*! You're just a little disillusioned suburbanite who doesn't realize you're also a target. You think just because you have light skin, light brown eyes, and curly long hair, it's going to save you."

The words stung like a slap. My features, the ones I'd inherited from my mother, thrown back at me as evidence of some supposed denial of my Blackness. These were the same features my grandfather had always regarded with a certain resigned disappointment whenever he looked at me too long. The same features that made strangers ask, "What are you?" with entitled curiosity.

Now Corey was weaponizing them against me in front of everyone as if my appearance alone was enough to invalidate my voice. I felt my hands trembling slightly, and I shoved them into my pockets. No one knew about the nights I'd spent staring in the mirror, searching for more of my father in my reflection, wondering if I had enough of him in me to belong.

"You're right, Co.! You're speaking the truth!" someone yelled.

"Black Lives Matter!" someone else yelled. This prompted more sounds of agreement, claps, and shouts of 'Black Lives Matter!'. The chant grew louder, surrounding me like a wave I couldn't swim against. My skin prickled with heat, sweat forming at the back of my neck as the circle seemed to close in.

My heart raced, feeling as if it could be seen pumping out of my t-shirt. I looked up at the eyes of those who stood around. Their lips contorted, their eyes squinted and glared, and their heads shook directly at me. I could hear my heart beating in my ears. I grabbed my chest. Not here, I thought. I took quick, deliberate breaths.

"Are you okay?" She reached her hand out.

"Fuck you!" I exploded and stormed off, pushing my way through the crowd. Words had failed me. The carefully constructed arguments I'd been so proud of moments ago were useless against the overwhelming need to escape.

As I walked up the lonely, dark, winding path toward my dorm, I felt hot. The buildings moved with each step I took. They grew taller, bending over me, their arms stretched out like they might swoop me up. I couldn't focus on one thing.

The campus I'd walked confidently through just hours ago had transformed into a threatening maze of concrete and shadow.

I heard the dog tags clinking beneath my shirt. I thought about my dad. The man I barely remembered but still carried with me everywhere, tied around my neck, close to my heart.

Maybe he would've told me to keep standing tall.

Even when it stung.

Even when it wasn't fair.

I bent over, sweaty palms resting on my knees, and released everything right there on the concrete. A splatter of everything I'd been trying to hold in stared back at me. My body had rejected what my heart couldn't take.

I kept walking. I was still boiling, my skin hot despite the night around me. The crisp evening air did nothing to cool me down.

Chapter Four

When I finally walked back into my dorm room, the matchbox space seemed even tighter and more confined than usual. The walls felt like they were pressing in, eager to hear about my humiliation.

My side of the room, plastered with photos of home, colorful tapestries, and scattered textbooks, contrasted sharply with my roommate's sterile half. Her side was all precision: desk organized with color-coded notes, bed made with hospital corners, a single motivational poster about perseverance hanging perfectly straight above it.

I looked at my roommate's empty bed and felt grateful once again that she was pre-med. She lived in the library. She had a dedication to her studies I had only ever witnessed with Asher.

I changed into my oversized, plush cotton shower robe and slides, grabbed my shower caddy and walked down the hall to our communal showers. The warm shower calmed my nerves.

When I got back to my room, I laid across my bed, picked up my cell phone and called Asher.

Outside of my mom, Asher knew me better than anyone else. We had been friends since the third grade, when he sat next to me at lunch. He just plopped down, startling me by slamming his lunch tray on the table. He didn't introduce himself or anything that would be considered polite or normal. He just pointed at my lip and said I had a red mustache from the juice I was drinking. My embarrassment was overcome by both his loud laughter and then my own.

Now, I lay across my bed in the dark, relieved that my roommate was still out. I needed to speak my mind without holding back.

"Yes, Ash, this girl really said that shit to me. She basically called me a—a—a sell-out. She called me a—a—a *disillusioned suburbanite*."

I heard Asher chuckle through the phone, his voice crackling slightly as it picked up a tinge of amusement. "Well, we did grow up in Willowbrook. That ain't Chicago like we be saying."

"What?" My eyebrows furrowed as the words stumbled from my mouth. I wasn't expecting that response from him. Asher had always been my sounding board, my echo, but lately, he'd been reflecting back truths I wasn't always ready to hear. Whenever we went anywhere, we'd tell folks we were from Chicago—the city.

I shifted on my bed, the cool sheets beneath me crinkling as I crossed my arms. The faint smell of the lavender-scented spray my mom had given me lingered in the air, a small comfort from home that suddenly made me feel both soothed and homesick all at once.

I only visited Chicago when I was with my grandfather, who lived in a wealthy, predominantly Black neighborhood there. He would drive out to our suburban home in Willowbrook to pick us up, then take us back to the city with him. We'd visit some family, or we'd go downtown to the museums, fancy restaurants, the Lakefront for walks along Lake Michigan, or to take rides on his huge sailboat my grandmother teased he loved more than her.

Willowbrook was not Chicago. Willowbrook was the complete opposite, with its quiet neighborhood of tree-lined streets and meticulously cut green grass that stretched out in front of Midwestern-style ranch homes in almost identical fashion. They stretched down each block you turned onto like little Monopoly houses lined up on the board. Pretty much all the major stores and businesses closed by 10 PM during the week *and* on weekends. But so what?

"So what if we're from the suburbs?" I said, returning my attention to Asher's voice on the line.

Willowbrook was a topic of great criticism for my grandfather. After my dad died, my mom moved us there from the city—a decision my grandfather never accepted. During pickups and drop-offs, he complained that our mom had moved us to the whitest suburb around. He argued she chose an area that was comfortable for *her* but didn't think of the Black children she was raising.

His voice echoed in my mind, a familiar blend of frustration and care: "And she just had to move y'all to one of the whitest suburbs around. Your father would have never stood for that!"

I blinked hard, shaking the thought off.

My grandfather had been right about one thing. There weren't a lot of Black kids at any of the schools I attended in Willowbrook, from elementary to high school. Not really much diversity at all. But I had Asher with me, and we did pretty much everything together.

It hadn't been all that bad, not even when I came home crying with a black eye after one of my teammates purposefully kicked the soccer ball into my face because she wanted to see if my eye would blacken or stay the same. That memory still stung; I could still taste the dirt mixed with the metallic tang of blood as I wiped my split lip.

My mother had told me to ignore ignorant people who were raised to believe "all of our blood wasn't red underneath our skin." So that's what I worked hard to do. Now, a couple of months into life at Franklin, these memories had started to resurface with new meaning.

Being at an HBCU was forcing me to see those past moments differently. Mom meant well, but was "ignoring" racism ever really possible for me? That advice came from a place her whiteness had protected—a privilege I couldn't fully share.

Back then, I'd just nodded and dabbed at my swollen lip, unable to name the disconnect. But here, surrounded by conversations about Blackness I'd only ever had at my grandfather's house, those old wounds were speaking a language I was only beginning to understand.

"She doesn't know me, Ash," I said now, my voice tight. 'Disillusioned suburbanite'? She's got some nerve! What if I called her a—a—a fake ass Angela Davis?"

Asher laughed out loud, "What? What is up with you and this girl?" His words were bright and easy, almost like he was lying back somewhere comfy.

"There's nothing 'up'." I snapped.

"Well, it seems like she likes picking arguments with you, Don."

"Right?"

"Yeah. And it seems like you like it, too."

I gasped, nearly dropping my phone. "What? No, I don't!"

"It's okay. Maybe you like the challenge. Maybe it turns you on a lil bit." His voice was heavy with mischief, his grin practically audible.

"No. No. No way. Now you're going too far!"

"Am I?" He asked, teasing me, like he could picture the incredulous look on my face.

"She's—she's, ugh!" I sighed, my fingers tightening around the phone like I could wring out my frustration. "Her shoes—they're all dirty and ran over. Her Afro is all over the place. She's always got on these cut-up shorts and shirts. Like she can never have on a regular shirt and pants! She's got all these friendship bracelets around her wrists like a schoolgirl, and—"

"And you like her," Asher blurted out. "Yes, *hon-ey*, you like this scraggly upperclassman who keeps calling you Freshy like she's a grad student or something. Don't you? Ahh-haa!! Yeesss!!" He laughed like he had solved a great mystery.

"Asher, stop it. Did you hear what I just told you she said about me?"

"Uh, I'm sorry, but in a way, she's right." His voice lost its playful edge, taking on the rare serious tone he reserved for when something really mattered. "When was the last time the news talked about a White person being murdered by the cops with their hands in the air?"

I was silent.

"Where the fuck do I fit in?" I finally mumbled, the words clawing their way out of my throat like they'd been trapped there since orientation day.

"Now that's your grandfather in your head again."

"No, Ash. It's not just about that. It's my whole life. My whole experience." I exhaled, feeling the weight of the words pressing against my chest. "I'm on this Black campus, surrounded by Black people, trying to find my place. Trying to find... myself." The last word slipped out in a whisper.

I had finally said it; spoken aloud the thing I had been holding back since I first stepped foot onto Franklin's campus. The truth was, Corey had only voiced what I already felt—what I feared most people were thinking.

That my light skin and the way I grew up gave me privileges that most Black people didn't have. That I was somehow confused about where I belonged, about how the world saw me. It was the very thing my grandfather had spent my whole life trying to make sure I never believed about myself.

My grandfather always emphasized with a certain seriousness, "You're Black, Chandon. Never forget that."

Asher's voice pulled me away from my thoughts. "Owning your Blackness and recognizing racism in America doesn't mean you're turning your back on your family—your mom." He fell silent.

"Ash?"

"I'm here. I was just thinking how this Corey girl got you thinking about some deep shit! Whoo!" he laughed.

"I don't even know why I allowed her to get to me. Everybody ain't gon' be marching up and down the street, Ash."

"You right, 'cause I ain't! Shit, why do you feel like you need to prove something to her? That's ya problem; you are always concerned about what this person and that person think about you.

I keep telling you to do you," he paused. "Or her." He laughed again like he'd just told the funniest joke in the world.

"Asher, stop it."

"I'm just saying, I'm your friend. Maybe this girl is good to have around." I could hear him smiling between words. "She's got you out there being social and trying new things, getting involved. Just work to change things in your own way. Do you. She can't tell you how to do that or what more you need to do. You got grandpops for that!" He laughed again.

I couldn't help but laugh too, a nervous, almost guilty chuckle. "That's for sure."

"Sooo, what's been up with you? How is Mr. Ivy League Extraordinaire?" I was happy to end the conversation about me.

"I don't know, Don." Asher's voice suddenly grew slower and quieter, his words hanging in the air like an unexpected storm.

Ever since I could remember, Asher had wanted to attend an Ivy League school. In high school, he'd filled up his resumé with service hours, extracurricular activities, and volunteering, all while maintaining stellar grades. He graduated as our school's valedictorian and was a member of The National Honor Society.

"What do you mean?" I asked, surprise making my voice crack. This wasn't like him. He should've been bragging about the fancy campus and how everyone was probably at his feet.

"I'm here. It's fine, but—" The phone went quiet. I pulled it back from my ear to check the connection.

Asher sighed, the sound heavy and deep, and I could hear the way it echoed off something on the verge of release.

"Honestly, I'm trying to find my place, too."

"And you will," I assured him. "Have you made friends? Joined any organizations or clubs? What about the honor society? Chess? You love chess!" Oh, great. Did I sound like my grandfather or what?

"Remember that time you invited me to your cousin's house on the southside?" he asked.

"Yeah," I said.

"Well, your cousin and I had what I thought was the strangest conversation at the time, but now I'm starting to see it differently. I think her name is Tanya, right?"

"Yeah, Tanya, that's her name. You know she got into UIC, right? What did she say to you?"

"She asked me questions like if I slept in my own bedroom," he continued. "If I lived with both of my parents, if I could hang out at the park in my neighborhood. She didn't ask me all at once, but she kept asking me these strange questions and I was so confused. I mean, yeah, she was nosy as hell," he chuckled. "But she was also trying to understand my world. To her, I lived in a different world."

"I mean, yeah, I guess."

I laid there staring up at the ceiling. It was strange how the worlds of Southside Chicago and Willowbrook could feel so far apart, and yet they were only miles away.

My grandparents had always made sure I spent time with my dad's side of the family. Tanya was nice, and fun, and played soccer with me. No, she didn't live with her father. But neither did I.

She slept in the room with her two younger sisters, and that was a pain when I spent the night, sure. But we always had fun together, and she never treated me like anything other than a cousin she enjoyed hanging out with.

And yet, Dad's family certainly acted differently from my mom's family—ate different foods and listened to different music. In their southside neighborhood, people hung out in their cars with the doors open and the music blaring old school songs, current R&B, or hip-hop from the trunks of their cars.

People sat on their front porches laughing and gossiping. Adults fussed after kids running through their grass or flower gardens from their porch or opened window. Cars sped down the street with people and music spilling out.

Kids played all kinds of games on the sidewalks: hopscotch, double-Dutch, and raced their bikes. It was rarely ever so quiet that you could hear the birds chirping or people-empty that you could see clear down the sidewalk to the end of the corner, like in my neighborhood in Willowbrook.

I welcomed the spark to my senses and the feeling being on the Southside gave me. It was like being wrapped in a warm, tight hug, or like eating a slice of apple pie fresh out of the oven.

"That's how I feel being here," Asher continued, bringing me back from my warm memories. "I feel like I'm in a different world. Like I don't fully understand this place. My classes aren't the problem. I just don't understand the people, and I don't think they understand me either.

"My classmates are driving BMWs and Range Rovers, using their parents' credit cards and shit—with no spending limits! I'm not legacy. My great-grandfather, grandfather, and dad didn't go here. I'm on a scholarship."

"Yeah, an academic scholarship! A full ride, because of your grades! You *earned* your spot, Ash."

He scoffed. "You know how many times I've had to say, 'No, I'm not an athlete. I'm not on the basketball team. I don't play any sport. You know how many times I've had to show my ID to campus security when it's dark outside? It's bullshit." He sighed.

"I don't fit in. I should have gone to Franklin. You were right." His voice had lost all of its usual confident swagger, replaced by something I rarely heard from Asher—uncertainty.

I sat up straighter on my bed, surprised. Asher had always been so sure of himself, so certain about his path. Hearing him doubt himself was like watching a lighthouse flicker out during a storm.

"Yeah, you should have," I jabbed, trying to lighten the mood despite the heaviness settling between us. "But seriously, this is your dream, Ash. "I paused. "BSU!" I blurted out. "Is there a BSU on your campus? I know there's got to be one." I cringed. What in the world was I saying?

"Now I've got to meet this Corey girl," he teased, sounding like himself again.

"Stop it, Ash! I'm serious. It might help."

"I love you, Don, but girl, you know that ain't even my thing! I don't need to be around a bunch of Black people to fit in. I already know I'm Black."

Ouch, I thought, the sharpness of his response settled deep in my chest.

"I've been thinking about joining the tech gaming academy or something. I'll figure it out. I just wasn't expecting this—to feel so lonely…so isolated."

"I know," I sighed, understanding exactly what he meant. The irony wasn't lost on me, both of us at our dream schools, both feeling like outsiders. "Ash?"

"Yeah?"

"Am I at this Black school trying to find my Blackness?" The question hung in the air, raw and exposed like a nerve. I could hear him take a deep breath on the other end—one of those long, slow ones that told me he was choosing his words carefully.

I imagined that maybe he was alone in his dorm room, too. I could almost hear the shift in his body language, the small movements as he adjusted himself, probably sitting at his desk in a worn-out chair or the edge of his bed.

"My bad, Don. I didn't mean it like that. I think—"

A knock at my door startled me. I sat up quick. I could almost feel the weight of the door as it vibrated from the knock.

"Hold on, Ash. I think this girl forgot her keys again."

I just knew it was my roommate. She'd forgotten her keys more times than I could count. I dragged my sock-covered feet over the cool, hard floor underneath me, sending a chill up my spine. I reached the door, the cold metal of the handle slightly cooler than I expected and opened it without bothering to ask who was on the other side.

My heart skipped a beat, and my eyes fluttered as I saw who was standing there, a mix of surprise and something else twisting in my stomach.

"Asher, I'll call you back." I spoke quickly into the phone.

"Wait. Who is that?"

I ended the call with a quick tap of my thumb.

"Hey." Corey stood there staring at me.

Time seemed to slow, my body registering her presence before my mind could catch up. My pulse quickened, a rush of something between anger and anticipation flooding my system.

"H—how did you find my dorm room?"

She chuckled. "You'll learn fast, Freshy. Nothing is a secret around here. Plus, I can figure out the answers to anything I need." She smiled and tapped her temple with an index finger.

I continued to stare. Her smile disappeared, and she cleared her throat.

"Chandon. I meant to say Chandon."

There she was, saying my name again, while I rode the wave of each sound as she released them from her lips, soft yet deliberate, like a slow exhale during meditation. She didn't say it like she said *Freshy,* with a lightness and playful tone. She said it with intention and depth, her voice settling into the space between us like the lingering warmth of a late summer evening.

I liked how her lips moved, shaping each syllable with a quiet precision, the faint sheen of gloss catching the dim light. And her eyes, deep, unblinking—traced my body as if mapping something familiar, something worth remembering. A shiver ghosted up my spine. I felt the hairs on my arm stand up as if drawn toward her, pulled by the gravity of her presence.

I managed to use my motor skills again, shoving my hands into my pockets.

"What's up," I said, trying to sound casual. My heart was beating like I was working out.

She cleared her throat. "I was wondering if you were free to take a walk with me."

"I'm actually, uh—" I turned to look at the crumpled-up blanket and dent my body left in my bed. "I've just got so much to do. Ho—homework."

Was she fucking serious? Why in the world would I want to take a walk with her? So she could embarrass me some more? Hell no.

"Listen, that was a lot. I know, I know. That was a lot. I'm sorry. Sometimes I—I just get so caught up in it." She shook her head. "I'm sorry."

"Yeah, it *was* a lot. Do you argue with everyone like that or just freshmen like me who you can embarrass?"

She dropped her head, looked up at me, and stepped inside the open door until we were inches apart. The scent of cocoa butter curled around me, warm and inviting. She placed her hand on my shoulder, her palm warm through the thin fabric of my shirt, the pressure light but grounding. The contact sent a ripple through me, like dropping a stone in still water. I focused on keeping my breathing even, on not leaning either toward or away from her touch.

"Honestly, Freshy, I didn't mean to embarrass you. Once I get going—" she shook her head, a flash of self-awareness crossing her features that I hadn't seen before. "It's just that my passion comes from a different place. That's why I'm here. I came here to apologize to you and explain myself."

"Thanks, but that won't change the fact that people gon' be looking at me like I'm a 'disillusioned suburbanite,'" I said, pulling my hands from my pockets to make air quotes, reminding her of her accusations about me.

"Where you grow up at?" She removed her hand from my shoulder, stepped back, and folded her arms.

"You don't know me," I said, still frowning.

"You right, I don't. That's why I'm here. I'm trying to get to know you."

"I thought you were here to apologize."

"Look, Freshy—"

"Chandon. My name is Chandon Elizabeth Kilpatrick."

She shook her head and licked her lips, the faint shine catching the light as her gaze traveled over me, slow and deliberate.

"You just—man, Fresh—" she cleared her throat, her voice dipping lower. "Chandon. There just aren't too many freshmen on campus like you. Hell, people. People on campus."

She was surveying my body again, her eyes moving with careful intensity, like she was trying to remember something. Like I was a thought on the tip of her tongue, just out of reach. I felt exposed and seen at the same time, in a way that made me want to both hide and step closer.

"Oh, so you go around picking fights with freshmen until you find the one who will stand up to you?"

"Nah. But I can just tell you're one of a kind."

My tongue rested in my mouth like a tree log.

She smiled. "I think you're—"

Before she could finish, the door creaked as someone pushed it open wider, the sound cutting through the charged air between us. I stepped back instinctively, suddenly aware of how close we'd been standing, feeling like I'd been caught doing something I shouldn't.

"Chandon, are you good? I told you to wait for me. You had me looking all around for you," Alisha said from the doorway, her voice edged with concern.

Her eyes flickered between us with a quick, calculating glance that she immediately masked, choosing instead to barrel forward with her agenda. "Somebody told me you got into an argument with one of the Hoteps on campus."

Corey sucked her teeth, tilting her head slightly in Alisha's direction as irritation flickered across her face.

"Oh, my bad. I didn't see you there!" Alisha turned her head toward Corey and then back toward me. "You guys busy, or you wanna go to the cafe? It's fried chicken Wednesday."

"I'm good. I'll catch up with you later, Chandon," Corey said, flashing that smile of hers. "If you give me your number, I can call you before I stop by next time."

She pressed her number into my phone and handed it back to me, her fingers brushing mine with a quiet heat. The brief contact felt deliberate, a promise of something unspoken.

"I'll be waiting. Enjoy the chicken," she said, her voice smooth, with a hint of amusement that danced in her eyes as she turned to leave.

"Damn, she thirsty, ain't she?" Alisha asked as soon as Corey was out of earshot.

"Girl!" I pulled her into my room and closed the door.

Chapter Five

After my public argument with Corey outside of Nash-Jamison Hall, I became known by many of my fellow Franklinites as the light-skinned girl who didn't think she was Black or simply as "All Lives Matter" or "Make America Great Again," which I fucking loathed!

My stomach would twist into knots whenever I caught fragments of these labels floating around me in the café or classroom. I didn't know a lot of things, but I knew for sure I wasn't voting for nor supporting that racist, sexist homophobe running for president.

The assumption that I would just because I questioned one aspect of social activism felt like the ultimate insult. Why was I even being associated with him? Because I had a different opinion—a different perspective? Yeah, Corey excited me, but she had embarrassed the shit out of me, too, and I was struggling to let it go.

In my English Literature class one afternoon, our professor was lecturing on Zora Neale Huston's short story, *Sweat*.

"In what ways can Zora Neale Hurston's *Sweat* be interpreted to resonate with the Black Lives Matter movement of today?" Dr. Collier asked.

Ebony raised her hand. "Well, for one, Delia is both Black and a woman, right? She's disrespected and abused, and everybody knows it, yet don't nobody do nothing to stop it from happening to her."

She was seated right next to me. There were murmurs and sounds of agreement from some of the other students, who sat in the two rows forming a semi-circle, with Dr. Collier standing smack dab in the center. Our young, eager faces stared back at her.

Dr. Collier had a strong presence, not just from her six-foot-tall frame but also from her large, perfectly round Afro. She gestured with her hands as she spoke, her gold bangles jingling around her wrists. Her words were slow and deliberate as if she thought over each one before they left her lips. She looked students directly in the eyes when she spoke to them.

Just above the white board at the front of the classroom was the only picture in the room. It was a rare colored picture of Zora Neale Hurston in a hat with a feather placed across its front, a fur draped across her shoulders. Her smile wide, her eyes hopeful. Underneath the picture was a quote from Hurston: "If you're silent about your pain, they'll kill you and say you enjoyed it."

Our class was small, with only twelve students, but we seemed to fill up the large square room with its big windows that revealed our campus's large trees and perfectly manicured lawn. On the opposite side of the room were two doors with square-shaped glass cut outs. One door was at the front of the class, and the other was at the back.

"Go on. Make your point," Dr. Collier urged Ebony.

Ebony was short and muscular; she was one of the stars on our track team. Her skin was dark and immaculately smooth, like the sun-kissed people of Sudan, and her white teeth spread across her face when she smiled, revealing two circled dimples in her cheeks.

In class, she seemed serious about everything. She held strong, heavy opinions, like almost everyone else at Franklin. Along with the ability to whip them out as easily as they said *good morning* or *how are you?* Did everyone have a grandfather training them for Franklin like I did? It sure seemed that way.

"Well," she licked her lips. I noticed how they glistened and moved when she spoke. I turned away quickly to avoid staring.

"Hurston explores the intersectionality of race and sex—nah, not sex, I mean gender. Delia has to live in both worlds—being Black and a woman. Dealing with both sexism and racism. Black Lives Matter directly speaks to the challenges Black women face and advocates for our visibility and rights alongside our fight for justice." She swooped her long, down-the-back cornrowed extensions over her shoulder with one motion and began to stroke her hair like it was a pet.

Sexy and smart. College was an amazing place, I thought.

"Something that wasn't done during The Civil Rights Movement," Tashia added in a matter-of-fact way.

"How so?" Dr. Collier perked up and walked toward the center of the open circle where Tashia sat.

Tashia, not backing down, sat up taller in her seat.

"Um, for one, during the Civil Rights Movement, Black women were literally forced into the background. They did so much work but received so little credit. Look at all the women of the movement we don't know about." She spoke directly at Dr. Collier.

Tashia was different; she wore six-inch heels, fitted skirts, and make-up. Her hair was always pressed and curled to her shoulders like she'd just stepped out of the beauty salon, and she smelled like she only wore the most expensive perfume. It was never overpowering, but she definitely made you turn and look at her after she passed by to figure out what it was that had excited your senses.

"Like who?" Jamal asked in a challenging tone. "We know about Rosa Parks—"

"Everybody *loves* throwing out Rosa Parks as an example!" Tashia rolled her eyes.

"I wasn't finished," Jamal shot back.

"Yeah, let the man finish." Andre said, he was seated right behind Tashia.

Tashia turned around, seeing a sly smile spread across his face, and said nothing. Andre had hazel eyes, deep three-hundred-and-sixty-degree waves printed into his freshly maintained haircut like one of the models for Murray's Pomade, and deep dark eyelashes that accentuated his eyes.

Whenever I saw him speaking to a girl on campus, he'd be licking his lips, smiling, leaning in and looking like he was attentively listening to her every word. A real lady's man type. He wasn't into the preppy look either, with his fresh black or white Air Force Ones, designer jeans, and crispy tees.

Jamal cleared his throat. "Like I was saying, we got Rosa Parks, but there are many others we know about. Septima P. Clark, Ella Baker, uh, Fannie Lou Hamer, and Diane Nash." He used a finger to count off each woman he identified.

"Jamal, you just learned about those women in this class!" Tashia shot back.

The room erupted in laughter. Even Dr. Collier had a slow smile spread across her face as if she was trying to hold it back or pretend like she hadn't been amused by the comment.

"Stop playing with me," Jamal groaned. "My grandfather was a Panther."

Everyone on campus knew this from day one since he practically led with that fact as if he was bragging about himself.

Jamal wore a suit and tie every day, even on Saturdays! He was the real serious type. He carried a briefcase, and it seemed like he had already mapped out his life's plan. Like he was just checking school off the list of things he would accomplish in life.

His wide nose, thick lips, and oversized ears made his head seem like it was smaller than it was, as if it was still growing into its facial features.

He wore oversized glasses which, to me, didn't help. But he was always seen walking around campus with a group of women. They could be seen talking and walking as if they weren't concerned about schoolwork and studying and were headed somewhere important. I guess the nerdy type was attractive in college. The opposite of what it was in high school.

Even if I was attracted to boys, he would not be my type, I told myself. Yet his confidence made me admire him.

Tashia hunched her shoulders. "You're proving my point, though. People, in general, don't know about these women. They aren't well-known like Rosa Parks. Stop it. People don't even know Fannie Lou Hamer is the reason Black people got the right to vote today. Or—or Nash was the leader of the freedom rides right here in this city!"

"There are plenty of men people don't know about either," Andre added.

Tashia turned all the way around towards him. "What's your point, Andre? Right now, we're talking about the *women*!"

"Calm down." He threw both hands up in the air.

She released a heavy sigh and turned back toward the front of the class, facing Dr. Collier.

"I—I don't think the women were pushed to the back of the movement," I said. It seemed like everyone in the room turned to look at me. Like Tupac, all eyes were on me. Even Dr. Collier stared at me.

"Okay. Go on," she encouraged.

"I think the women understood their strength but played the hand society gave them to see to it that forward progress was made. It was a smart move. The best move. The move that allowed us to win. Black women lead many movements, but they couldn't be the face at the front because society wasn't ready for that. So, they supported the men who could do it.

"Like Delia in the story, she played her part, kept working hard and allowed Sykes to believe he was in control. If she had done anything more, the town would have blamed her more than they already did. She could have been killed. In the end, she got her freedom." I sat back and folded my arms.

"You would say that," Ebony chirped. "All Lives Matter," she mocked.

The class erupted in laughter.

"We will have none of that, Ms. Davidson." Dr. Collier's voice cut through the noise with sharp precision.

Ebony dropped her head like a scolded puppy. The laughter ceased immediately. To my surprise, Jamal—Mr. My-grandfather-was-a-Panther himself—cleared his throat loudly.

"Hold up," he said, adjusting his glasses with an unexpected gentleness that contradicted his usual stiffness. "She's actually making a strategic point worth considering. The movement was about achieving results, not just making statements."

Tashia raised an eyebrow at him, twisting a strand of her perfectly styled curls around her finger. "Since when you defend anyone who isn't quoting Malcolm X verbatim?" There was genuine curiosity beneath her challenge, not just antagonism.

"Since we're supposed to be having an actual intellectual conversation," Jamal replied, a flash of vulnerability crossing his usually composed face. "My grandfather also taught me to listen before dismissing someone's perspective entirely."

Andre leaned forward in his seat, his usual smooth demeanor shifting to something more thoughtful. "Man, my auntie used to say the same thing about her time marching. Said sometimes the men got to stand in front because they'd take the first blows from the police." He shook his head slightly, his hazel eyes focused on some distant memory. "But she was always there, making plans, sending letters, organizing behind the scenes."

"Let's unpack some of you all's points. First, I think Ms. Kilpatrick brings up some concepts worth exploring. What would have happened had the women demanded from the men equal positioning and visibility during the fight for freedom and equality?

"Would the movement still have been successful? Would it have taken longer to accomplish the goal, or would it have been accomplished in less time? Think about the zeitgeist of the time, as Ms. Kilpatrick mentioned."

Although Dr. Collier validated my input, the damage was done. I was reminded yet again of the impact that argument with

Corey had on my reputation around campus. I shut down and didn't speak for the remainder of the class.

I tried to rush out using the back door when we were dismissed. Just as my feet were crossing the threshold, I heard Dr. Collier call me back into the class.

"One moment, please, Ms. Kilpatrick."

I sighed and paused. *Should I pretend I hadn't heard her*, I thought. *No. Hell no.* I shook that idea away. Professors were known for showing up at your dorm room without warning for skipped classes or to provide parent-like lectures. I turned around, bumping into Ebony as she walked out of class. Our eyes locked, but neither one of us uttered a word. I walked toward the front of the class, my heart pounding.

I stood in front of Dr. Collier's antique brown wooden desk that looked like it had been in the class as far back as the Civil Rights Movement. It looked well used, with marks and dents all over the top. She sat behind it and looked at me with those dark, piercing eyes of hers.

"You have a strong voice, Ms. Kilpatrick." I lifted my head at her words. The validation felt foreign—almost uncomfortable—after days of being reduced to the "All Lives Matter girl."

"Yes, you heard me correctly. Everyone won't always agree with you and may even use fallacious argumentative tactics to silence you. Will you let them?" She paused. "That is the question. Learn to be prepared and ready for all types of rebuttals. Do you understand?" She didn't blink as she looked at me.

"I—Y—yes." I reluctantly shook my head.

"Good. Then another day like today won't happen in my class, right?"

I frowned and looked to my left and right. "Like what?" I asked as if I was really confused.

She picked up the pile of papers that rested on her desk in front of her. Papers each one of us had put there earlier when we walked in at the beginning of class. A ten-page, twelve-point font, Times New Roman, double-spaced paper on the symbolism in *Sweat*. She began stacking and organizing the collected papers on her desk, her movements precise, as if I were no longer standing there.

I reluctantly shook my head. She stopped shuffling the papers, her eyebrows raising as she squinted at my non-verbal reply. I quickly straightened my posture.

"No. No, it won't, Dr. Collier." I swallowed hard.

She gave a half smile. "See you in class on Thursday, Ms. Kilpatrick." She continued packing away the papers on her desk into her brown leather bag.

You have a strong voice, Ms. Kilpatrick. Dr. Collier said it as if she meant it, too. Not like she was trying to convince me that it was true. What did she mean when she said people would try to silence me? People wouldn't have to try to silence me if I silenced my damn self. I've got to do better, I told myself.

My grandfather would not have been proud of me for shutting down like that in the middle of the class discussion. He never let me walk away from a debate, conversation, or argument with him. I always had to defend my position no matter how emotional I got. Yet, so far, I had stormed off from one argument and shut down in another. Zero for two.

Outside Nash-Jamison Hall, I paused beneath the shade of a massive oak tree, my backpack suddenly feeling twenty pounds heavier. The afternoon sun filtered through the leaves, casting shifting patterns on the brick path below. A few students lounged on the grass nearby, their laughter drifting across the yard.

I leaned against the rough trunk, letting the bark press against my back as I closed my eyes, replaying the classroom scene in my head. Despite the surprising support from Jamal and Andre, all I could hear was Ebony's mocking tone and the laughter that followed. It was as if my ears were tuned only to rejection, filtering out everything else.

"Girl, you coming or what?" Alisha's voice broke through my thoughts. She stood a few feet away, head tilted, an expression of mild concern crossing her face. "I've been waiting for you."

"Yeah, sorry." I pushed off from the tree, adjusting my backpack strap. "Just thinking."

"Well, don't think too hard. You might hurt yourself." She grinned, linking her arm through mine as we began walking.

We walked back to the dorms together. Instead of taking the sidewalk, we chose the cobblestone road, which was closed to traffic years ago. The stones beneath our feet uneven and worn smooth by decades of students before us.

The library stood like an aging guard, its brick facade weathered but dignified, windows reflecting the afternoon sun like knowing eyes that had witnessed generations of students pass through its doors.

As we passed it, students trickled in and out—books in hand, backpacks strapped to their shoulders. Some walked carefree on cheap dates with their fingers intertwined, while others simply soaked in the quiet calm of campus at night. Even with the sun going down, the historic buildings loomed over us, their fortress-like presence both protective and eerie.

She broke our silence. "Girl, I got yo' back."

"Oh, yeah? How?"

"Well, passing the library made me remember I got some tea to spill. I was standing in line checking out a book for Dr. Mitchell's class when I heard ol' gossiping-ass Sierra talking to this other girl—I don't know her name, but I've seen them hanging tough together lately. She's short and dark-skinned." Alisha held her hand up to show the girl's height. "They say she run track. You probably don't know her."

Was she referring to Ebony, I wondered. The thought lingered for a moment before I shrugged it away. I didn't have the energy to ask.

"Anyway," she continued, "I heard Sierra saying that you were just pretending to be White for attention, girl! Can you believe that? Like, who pretends to be White for likes?"

"Wow," was all I could muster. The word barely made it past my lips, weighed down by the lump forming in my throat.

It had been weeks since that confrontation on the yard, but whispers, stares, and rumors still clung to me like the sticky Southern heat. I hated Corey for that.

Freshman year was all about perception—about being sized up, labeled, and sorted into categories people could understand. If you landed in the wrong one, good luck climbing out.

Get caught leaving a boy's room too late? You were a hoe. Not the boy, though. Just the girl. Miss a few too many classes? A slacker. A nobody.

And if you spent too much time in the campus cyphers, rocking an Afro or Locs, dissecting the world with a little too much intensity? You were one of them—labeled a Hotep, militant, overzealous, too deep for your own good. Like Corey.

"I set her ass straight for you, though. I told her that she needed to mind her own damn business and stop talking about people she didn't know."

"Thanks, Lish." I sighed, the weight of it settling in my chest. "I guess I'm like the Black Rachel Dolezal around here, huh?" I let out a dry laugh. The words felt strange even as I said them, like I was trying to make a joke out of something that wasn't funny at all.

Alisha slapped my back, the impact jolting through me as she bent over in a deep, chesty laugh. It rolled out of her in waves, full-bodied and unrestrained, lasting long enough to seep into my bones until I found myself laughing, too.

Although I didn't think it was funny, her laughter was contagious, filling the space between us and smoothing out the sharp edges of my thoughts. It wrapped around me like an embrace I hadn't realized I needed, warm and steady, grounding me in a moment that, for once, didn't feel so heavy. I wiped tears of laughter from my eyes with both hands, my breath still uneven.

"I'm serious."

"Nah, girl. You really *are* Black and White. That woman took cultural appropriation to a whole other level! Rachel Dolezal." She shook her head and chuckled some more. "Girl, stop! You are too funny for that one!"

What Alisha didn't know, and what I wasn't sure she'd understand if I told her, was that I really did feel lost in my own identity. I wasn't White enough for White people, and I wasn't Black enough for Black people. I was somewhere in the middle of a vortex that felt lonely and isolating as hell, like standing in a crowded room while no one could really see me.

I wondered if my dad ever felt this split. Caught between worlds that didn't see the whole of him. Maybe that's why I clung so hard to the stories about him. To the pictures. To the promises I could still feel under my skin, even if I didn't have the full memory to match.

The feelings rose up uninvited, each one a piece of the puzzle I couldn't quite solve. The weight of it sat heavy in my chest, pressing down like thick, humid air before a storm. Some days, it felt like I was spinning, caught between two worlds that both questioned me, measured me, and found me lacking. Other days, it was just a quiet emptiness, a space I couldn't quite fill no matter which way I turned.

I thought things would be different at Franklin. Maybe this was what my grandfather had been trying to prepare me for—to mold me into my Blackness. But even with my dad's family, a piece of me felt like I did at Franklin. Like I was looking in from the outside, pressing my hands against the glass but never quite stepping through.

My grandfather said it like a warning: *never forget you're Black.* He often pointed out that I didn't know the language fully. I put emphasis on the wrong words, my tongue stumbling where theirs flowed with ease. I didn't fit, I didn't have the style down—wasn't effortlessly cool, the way my cousins seemed to just *know* what worked.

The inside jokes sometimes missed me, laughter swelling around me while I tried to catch up. And my dance moves? Off. I was usually two steps behind, too busy thinking about the steps ahead instead of listening and *feeling* the beat, the rhythm pulsing beneath my feet.

"Girl, that lack of rhythm come from yo' White side!"

"You ain't never heard this song? How?"

"What do you mean your mama puts breadcrumbs on top of the macaroni?"

"Raisins don't go in potato salad, chile, please!"

Each comment landed like a playful jab, but I felt every single one of them, small reminders that I never quite fit no matter where I was. Being Black seemed to be something that was just *understood* in the way everything was done. A look, a tone, a movement, each carried an unspoken language, and you either knew it or you didn't.

Having to have something naturally understood explained to you often came with ridicule, laughter, or an exasperated burden in the tone of the explainer: *I can't believe I have to explain this to you.*

"Being Black is rich like Mississippi soil and sweet like molasses, baby girl. It's a cultural experience you gotta be emersed in it. That's why it's important you two are around your family," my grandfather stressed. "And I'm going to make sure of that," he said, his words heavy with promise.

With my mom and her side of the family, things were straightforward. Plain. Simple. Easy to understand. Direct. Things were what they were. We played cornhole and swam at family barbecues. We laughed and talked, but never loud enough for the sound to carry from the front of the house to the back.

"Indoor voices, Chandon," my mom would remind me if I got too excited, her hand gently squeezing my shoulder as a warning. "We're not at a football game."

"Elizabeth, let the child be a child," my maternal grandfather Payne would say, but even his protest came in measured tones, like a suggestion written in a polite email.

We sang from our hymn books on Sunday. Three songs every Sunday. Nothing more, nothing less. The preacher didn't scream and shout, didn't pat the running sweat from his forehead with a handkerchief after every drawn-out syllable backed by the organ. No one had a reason to pass out and be ushered back to their seat by women in white outfits with matching gloves.

"That's quite enough," my maternal grandmother—grandma Ethel, once whispered when we visited a Baptist church with my dad's parents. "All this... performance. I don't see how anyone can hear the word of God through all this commotion."

After church let out three hours after it started, she mumbled under her breath on the way out the door that it would be her first and last visit.

When we went to church with them and my mom, it was over in time to watch Sunday football and eat dinner together.

In the summer, I went camping with my grandma Ethel and grandpa Payne and learned how to start a fire; the sharp snap of twigs beneath my hands, the scent of smoke curling into the air as flames took shape was exhilarating.

We talked about school, sports, TV shows, and other light-hearted topics of conversation. No one sat around debating issues of race or how being White impacted their lives. If they did, I was never around for those conversations.

I was thirteen when I began to feel the cultural whiplash. After a weekend at my grandfather's, where I'd been immersed in heated debates about politics and identity, I returned to Grandma Ethel's and Grandpa Payne's house for Sunday dinner feeling electric, alive with new ideas.

"Did you know," I announced, fork jabbing the air, "that the history textbooks just completely skip over—"

"Chandon," my mother cut in, her eyes darting to my grandparents. "Maybe save the heavy topics for after dessert?"

Later, in the car, she explained: "Some conversations aren't dinner appropriate."

I stared out the window, confused. At my grandfather's house, no conversation was too big for the dinner table. There, not talking was what was inappropriate.

I began to understand then that I lived in translation, constantly recalibrating my voice, opinions, and my very self, depending on which side of my family I was with.

The handoffs of me and my brother were always tense. Mom would pull up to the curb, never turning off the engine. My grandfather would come to the door but rarely past the threshold.

"Elizabeth," he'd acknowledge with a curt nod.

"Emanuel," she'd respond, her voice neutral but her knuckles white on the steering wheel.

Once inside my grandparents' home, talks about race were as natural as talking about the weather. Woven into everyday moments, slipping into conversations over dinner, in the car, during commercial breaks. It was never a question of if race would come up, only when.

"Baby girl, you see that?" My grandfather would point to the TV, where a Black man was being interviewed. "You watching? That's what excellence looks like. That's us right there."

"Honey, she knows," my grandmother would say, but there was pride in her voice too.

"She better know," my grandfather would reply. "This world won't let her forget she's Black, but they sure will try to make her forget she's excellent. Just like your daddy was."

The mention of my father would hang in the air, his absence was a presence all its own.

If someone committed a crime or some other illegal offense that made the news, someone would ask without hesitation, "Were they Black?"

If they were, a heaviness settled over the room, unspoken but felt. It was as if everyone carried a piece of the awareness of how this would be used against us all.

"Media going to run with this for weeks," my uncle would say, rubbing his temples. "Meanwhile, where are the perpetual positive images of us flooding the screens?"

If they weren't Black, there was a collective sigh of relief, a quiet release of tension.

"Y'all see how they aren't saying anything about his race?" my aunt would say. "If he was Black, that'd be the headline."

One day, my aunt was talking about work with a friend she had brought to one of my grandfather's famous cookouts. They were seated on swivel stools at the massive butcher block-style island. Though it was the centerpiece of the kitchen, there was still plenty of space for a large group to gather, as we often did.

Aunt Sharonda was going on about a woman at work who had filed some court documents incorrectly.

"For the umpteenth time," I heard her say.

When my aunt called her out on it, she said the woman started crying.

"You know how they do. They love—" She turned then, her eyes landing on me where I stood at the farmhouse-style sink in front of the garden window.

I was rinsing dishes and loading them into the dishwasher while watching my younger cousins toss the football around in the backyard grass.

"Hey, Don. Go tell your uncle to come here, please."

I stopped and dried my hands on the dish towel. "Okay."

As I walked out, closing the screen door behind me, I heard my aunt finish her sentence.

"Crying those White woman tears."

Her friend agreed, "Mm-hmm. Girl, you know it. No account-ability."

I felt my heart sink. Why didn't my aunt think it was okay to say that in front of me? I *knew* I belonged in that world because it was just a fact. I was indeed Black. That was for sure. But I wanted to *feel* it without question.

Chapter Six

I had been going to Dr. Collier's office hours ever since that day in her class. Her words stuck with me: *You have a strong voice, Ms. Kilpatrick.* And although she intimidated the hell out of me with her piercing, deep eyes and direct questions, her office was one of the few places outside of my dorm room where I felt completely safe.

At first, I stopped by for help with my papers before I submitted them. But soon, our conversations evolved, reminding me of those I had with my grandfather, only hers weren't riddled with constant criticism. She made me feel like a leader, pointing out the strength in my voice, both in my written assignments and during class discussions.

I grew more comfortable, realizing that I enjoyed speaking my mind and sharing my opinions. The more I visited her, the more she encouraged me—to *read more, study more, and speak up more in class.* So, I did.

I was leaving for another office visit with Dr. Collier. This time, our conversation took a sharp turn when she said she wanted to see me put my knowledge and all I had inside me into action.

"You know, students like you are usually very active on our campus," she said, peering over her thick-rimmed glasses at me. Her maroon lipstick accentuated her full lips.

I just sat there and sighed. The words hung in the air between us, heavy and unexpected. The quiet hum of her office fan suddenly seemed louder, and the space between us charged with an expectation I hadn't seen coming. My fingers tightened around the strap of my backpack, the fabric rough against my skin.

"You have a powerful mind, Ms. Kilpatrick. Use it!" Her tone was right on the cusp of demanding.

I sat frozen, her words echoing in my head. A part of me wanted to ask, "How?" but another part feared what that would commit me to. I'd come to her office seeking safety, not marching orders. The weight of her expectation pressed against my chest as I gathered my things.

I walked across campus, ignoring the shouts and stomps of the sororities and fraternities in individual lines and formations, moving in lock step with their rehearsed choreography.

The ladies of various organizations—in their red and white, pink and green, blue and white, and blue and gold jackets, shouting their group's call and response above the blaring music—had me fixated on them when I first arrived on campus. They looked so powerful and forceful. They demanded my attention.

Folks were gathered around them, cheering them on, talking, laughing, and dancing, but I rushed past them. It was one of those fall days, right in the middle of the hot summer, saying goodbye and the hint of cold weather on the way, saying; *here I come, enjoy it while it lasts!*

Change was in the air. The leaves seemed to fall from the trees with the stomping and fervor of those repping their organization. I wanted to stop and enjoy the vibe, but I wavered between feeling betrayed and feeling empowered. Dr. Collier had welcomed me into the safety of her office only to abruptly push me out like a baby bird from its nest.

Was I ready? And what exactly did she want me to do? Or rather, what was I going to do? Here I was once again hearing the call to do more, but this time, I also felt it inside of myself. I both admired her and felt duped all at once.

My unsettled emotions made me tired. My legs felt hollow beneath me; each step unsure as if testing new wings, I wasn't convinced would hold me.

I raced to my room, where I planned to remain hidden for the rest of the day. My roommate was just leaving when I made it to our room. She offered to give me a ride with her to the store to stock up on snacks and other personal items. I quickly declined.

Instead of taking a nap, I put my pent-up energy to work. I spread my textbooks across my bed, the African American Literature syllabus glaring up at me. Three papers due in the next two weeks, and I'd barely started the reading. Dr. Collier expected excellence, and I wanted to deliver. She saw something in me that I was still learning to see in myself.

My grandfather had always pushed me to speak up, but I felt he wanted me to echo his thoughts and perspectives. This was different. This was about finding my own voice, my own causes.

I highlighted passages in Hurston's text, seeing connections between her words, Black Lives Matter, and *Demand to Be Safe & Gay*. I began to see more clearly that academics and activism weren't so separate after all. I realized I had a lot more to learn.

Chapter Seven

Alisha walked right in without knocking on the door. She closed the door and turned the lock behind her like *she* was my roommate. Although I'd wanted a moment to decompress and think, I was happy to see her.

I leaned on my elbows as she plopped down at the foot of my bed. Her butt pressed against my feet as she sat.

"What's up, Lish?"

"Why are you cooped up in here like a hermit when everybody and they mama is on the yard right now?"

I shrugged and hopped out of bed. I pulled out the chair to my desk, turned it around, and faced Alisha. She slid down the bed so close to me that our knees grazed each other's.

"You don't hear that? It's cracking out there!"

I could hear the bass thumping from the speakers playing music outside.

"What's up? What's going on?" She lightly pushed her knee into mine.

I noticed the clear coat of polish shining on her nails. They were perfectly manicured and evenly shaped, round and cut low. Her lips were always glistening with some shade of pink or red lip gloss. She wore jeans that hugged the curves of her thick thighs and round hips. And she almost always had on a fresh pair of J's on her petite feet.

Her wrinkle-free t-shirts carried one designer's name or another, right below three to four sparkling gold chains. Her skin was camel leather brown and smooth. And I liked the low fade, curly top style of her hair; its mahogany color matched her skin and accentuated her round, lightly freckled face.

I leaned my head to one side as I paid more attention to her than I ever had. She carried herself with a confidence I both envied and admired, like someone who never questioned whether she belonged here. While I was still trying on different versions of myself, Alisha seemed to have arrived fully formed, unapologetically herself from day one. I wondered if it was just who she'd always been.

"Alisha, where are you from?"

She looked down at her black and red high-top Air Jordans and crossed one leg over the other.

"Chi-town, baby. Of course! Don't act like you can't tell!" she said it proudly. "What about you?" She gave a chin up head nod in my direction. "What suburb you from?" She paused and waited.

"How are you just going to assume I'm from the suburbs? I see you listening to these rumors out here," I smirked.

"Girl, never that. I peep your vibe. I can just tell." Her eyes seemed to tighten and roam my body as she sized me up.

I perked up and cleared my throat. "Like what," I said. "What about me says suburbs?"

She chuckled. "Well, that for one." She leaned back on my bed on her elbows, legs still crossed. "Ain't nobody from any major city trying to convince you they are from where they say they from. Believe them or not; they'll show you better than they can tell you anyway."

I bit my bottom lip and shook my head. "I can see that."

"Well?"

"Well, what else?"

"Okay. You are going there, I see. The way you speak. Super proper-like most of the time. Pronouncing every fucking syllable." She overexaggerated each sound with her cherry glossed lips.

"Not that people from the city don't speak proper English, it's just that yours seems so clean and unrehearsed—authentic, brought up, natural. There's no effort to it for you. You're not code switching. The way you walk, even. I don't see you ever looking around or checking your surroundings. You look like you're so sure you're safe.

"And you seem to care so much about what other people think of you, too much even. You see me? I don't give a fuck what these folks think. I'm here. And that's the attitude most of us from the city have because ain't nobody expect us to be here in the first place."

"Shit. That's deep, Lish." I said it slowly, letting the weight of her words settle in. She'd just revealed to me things I'd never really thought about.

"So—" She sat up, uncrossed her legs and leaned into me, her elbows resting on her knees and her left hand covering her right hand, which was balled into a fist. "'Burb now, please?" She said it in a tone that was lower and sweeter. I felt the soft air from her breath brush across my face.

"Willowbrook." The name barely left my tongue before the smile spread across her face.

She placed her hand on my knee. "There's nothing wrong with where you're from. Embrace it. I like that about you." The last of her words were in that same low, sweet tone again.

I felt a warm sensation come over me. I stared at her hand resting on my knee, heat pooling beneath her touch, my skin suddenly hyperaware of its weight.

"I can learn a few things from you because you're not from where I'm from, and you can learn some things from me, too. It's the beauty of why we're here, ain't it? Getting to know people from different places. It's all good!" She winked at me.

That warm feeling trickled throughout my body again. This time, landing right between my opened thighs. I was startled by my own reaction. What was that? The same flutter I'd felt around Corey, now happening with Alisha. I pushed the thought away, unprepared to examine what it might mean. I closed my legs quickly, then stood up. Alisha stood up, too.

"So, what we 'bout to do?" She didn't wait for my response. "We out. Let's go mingle on the yard and see what's up."

Once I was out of my room and out of my head, I was grateful to Alisha for stopping by. My wide smile and laughter came to a halt as soon as I saw Corey approaching us. But the butterflies and the quick, pulsating sensation swirling through my chest, could not be ignored. I hated how my body betrayed me around her—angry at her one moment, breathless the next.

Part of me wanted to grab Alisha's arm and bolt in the opposite direction. Another part wanted to stand my ground, to prove I wasn't intimidated. And a third part, the part I was least willing to acknowledge, simply wanted to be near her again.

I noticed she had those busted-up Chuck Taylors on again, joggers that sagged off her butt because they were too big. She had the legs pulled up to reveal her runner's calves on both sides, and a *Franklin University Athletics* t-shirt with the sleeves cut off, showing off the muscles in her arms.

Her 'fro was freshly cornrowed in individual braids flowing to the back, no extensions. They reached the nape of her neck and were rolled in small balls at the end with black rubber bands. The complete opposite of Alisha, I caught myself thinking.

"Ain't that your Hotep friend?" Alisha jabbed.

I gave her a side eye, slow and deliberate, my brow slightly raised as if to say, *Really?* Corey's fragrance met me before she did. I instinctively inhaled her scent, the delicate mix of cocoa butter and vanilla, sharp yet alluring, with a hint of something deeper, tugging at me in a way I couldn't ignore. I could almost taste it on my tongue, sweet and familiar.

"Hey, Freshy," she smiled.

I felt my heart sink, the weight of it settling like a soft sigh in my chest. My body and mind were in perfect disagreement, one leaning toward her, the other pulling away. The contradiction felt exhausting, like trying to walk in two directions at once.

"What are you doing here?" I blurted.

"Well, hi to you, too." She looked at Alisha. "Y'all headed to the yard?"

"Yep." Alisha said, a curtness to her tone.

"Oh, I see. My bad." She stepped back.

"No. No, no, no." I saw myself reach out for her wrist to stop her from walking away. It was instinctive, before I could even think about what I was doing. She looked down at my hand and gave a sly smile. Then she lifted her glasses up on her nose with the index finger of her other hand. I noticed the black tape still wrapped around the handle.

I cleared my throat. "Alisha, this is Corey. Corey, this is Alisha," I said, looking between them both. They greeted each other with hellos and faint smiles.

"BSU president, right?" Alisha asked.

"Yes, that's me," Corey stood a little taller. "We meet tomorrow at six. Feel free to stop by." Corey smiled at her.

"Thanks for the invite." She shifted her body weight to one side and stared at me. "So, are we going on the yard or what?" Alisha urged more than asked.

"Actually, I need to—to speak with Chandon for a minute. If you don't mind." Corey smiled.

I swallowed, the knot in my throat going down slow. "I-I'll meet you out there, 'Lish."

"Cool. Text me when you're done." I watched her walk away.

"That's your friend?" Corey glanced back at Alisha.

"Yeah, why?" I frowned at the question.

"Yeah, right. I'm your friend, too, then." she smirked.

"No, you're not." I pressed my right hand into my chest for emphasis. *"My friends* wouldn't pick an argument with me and embarrass the shit out of me in front of the whole damn school."

"It wasn't the whole school. Come on, stop exaggerating. And I apologized for that!" Her voice was slightly raised in agitation.

I felt my heart race as I looked around, my eyes wide with fear and concern. "Are you going to do it again?"

She put her hands up. "No. No. My bad."

I cleared my throat. "It sure does feel like the whole school. You got people walking around calling me *All Lives Matter.* That's fucked up, Corey." I felt a surge of pride as I released the words.

"Nah. Uh-uh, Freshy. *You* got people calling you that. Not me."

"You're something else." I sighed and shook my head. "I'm done."

I began to walk away. She reached for my arm. "What?" I asked, staring at the place on my arm where she held me.

She stood there for a moment looking at me, something dancing in her eyes as they searched mine. The silence between us loud.

"Okay, well, I'm here once again, hoping we can move past all that. If—if—if you walk away, I'm not coming back." I noticed a slight tremble in her lips.

"Good." I couldn't stop myself. She pushed past me with a fury.

My feet felt rooted to the ground, caught between following her and letting her go. Relief and regret battled inside me. Relief that I'd finally stood up for myself. Regret that I'd shut down whatever olive branch she might have been extending. I exhaled slowly, uncertain if I'd just won or lost.

Don't turn around, don't turn around, I pleaded with myself. I felt my phone buzzing in my pocket. I pulled it out immediately.

I checked. Our fall breaks align! Thank God! I told my folks I'm not coming home. I need a REAL break. I'll be there on Saturday. Flight already purchased. Be ready, bitch! (dancing emoji, dancing emoji, dancing emoji)

It was from Asher. Yes! My mood instantly lifted. Just like that, Corey was the last thing on my mind. Thoughts of her scattered from my mind like autumn leaves in a quick gust of wind.

Asher was coming! My day one. The only person who really got me. With him here, I wouldn't have to face all this Franklin drama by myself. Finally, someone who knew the real me, not whatever version of me people here had made up in their heads.

HESTER
HOUSE

Chapter Eight

A few days later, I was happy to be at an ACU meeting. I hadn't seen or heard from Alisha. I was hoping to catch her at the meeting since she'd never missed one. I came early, hoping to connect with her before we got started.

The updated, purple painted craftsman style door chimed each time it opened. The soft electronic tone bounced off the wooden floors and high ceilings, creating a ritual of anticipation with each person who entered.

The house smelled of lemon furniture polish and old books, a combination that had become oddly comforting over the past few weeks. I sat on the couch facing the door and picked up a WNBA magazine from the coffee table to occupy my mind as I waited.

The cover featured two former Franklin grads, Taylor M. Dawson and Raquel Williams. The glossy issue showed them mid-celebration, championship confetti raining down as they held the trophy between them. They were only the seventh and eighth players from an HBCU to play in the league and the first two to win a title. Our school beamed and bragged with pride about them.

"Hey. Chandon, right?" He said it like he already knew the answer.

I looked up to see our president, Chris Ford, standing in front of me. Even smiling, he always had a seriousness about him. Chris was tall, frail, and light complexioned. He kept a low, even haircut, the style my grandad always got my younger brother when he took him to the barbershop with him.

A number two fade, my grandfather said, was a Black boy's style, not the naturally golden-brown curls my mom let his hair grow into. The first time we came back home from visiting my grandparents' house with his hair freshly cut like this, my mom cried and said he looked like a little version of my dad.

Chris stood straight up; there was no bending or slouching in his posture. That, along with his gold round wire-framed eyeglasses, plaid tucked-in shirts, khaki pants, and penny loafers, made him look like a modern-day urban Steve Urkel—not Stephon.

Did he have a million of the same outfits or did he wash the same ones over and over? I pondered every time I saw him.

"Hey, Chris." I smiled back. "Guilty as charged."

"How are things going for you around here?"

I cleared my throat. "Well, um—"

"You can be honest. This is a safe space. Here, let me sit." He hiked his pants up before he sat down. His argyle socks showed.

He sat close enough that our knees touched slightly. I looked at his cream-colored khakis touching my blue jeans, unsure of where to focus my eyes.

"Oh, I'm sorry." He scooted over just far enough that our bodies no longer touched. "You want to speak in the other room, where I can close the door?" he asked.

"Why?"

"So, you can speak freely, of course. Although, you know, we are seated in the room dedicated to C.J. Malcolm, where everyone is *safe* and free to speak their truth. As part of our membership and access to this house, this room is a sacred space." He looked up to the ceiling and around the room.

I nodded and smiled.

"Well?" He looked at me closely, then down at my tapping foot, then back towards me, and pushed his eyeglasses up on his face.

"Being bullied by any group of people for any reason is unacceptable, Chandon." He waited. "We can't uplift one group of oppressed people while tearing down anybody else." His tone was serious and direct.

I nodded slowly.

"I heard about what's been happening to you around campus. It's unacceptable. You're allowed to speak your truth and have your opinions without being called out of your name."

I sighed and looked away.

"So, you know what I'm talking about, then?" He paused. "You're not the first student to have a run-in with Corey. She means well, but she can be over the top. Past the point of passionate, sometimes, in *my* opinion." He emphasized the word *my* by touching his chest.

"We came in together, you know, Corey and me. We've had our fair share of clashes both on the yard and in classes. She has a deeper story—a tragedy, really." He shook his head at the thought. "A trauma that fuels her passion and doesn't allow her to see widely enough. You know?" He looked at me like I knew what the hell he was talking about.

I didn't know—but I shook my head anyway and wondered what tragedy he was talking about. I was curious as hell, but something about the way his voice got all serious made me hold back from asking. Whatever had happened to Corey was clearly her business to share. I rubbed my arms even though I wasn't cold and looked around at the students who had started to trickle in.

"Listen," he lowered his voice. "If Corey is bullying you—"

I frowned. "She's not bullying me."

"She's not doing anything to stop the rumors either, is she?"

"What is she supposed to do?"

"She knows what the hell she's supposed to do. People around here listen to her. Some even worship her," he scoffed. "You shouldn't be dealing with any type of bullshit because of her." He was no longer whispering, and my eyes darted around the half-filled room.

"Sorry," he said, lowering his voice to a whisper.

He touched my shoulder, then removed his hand. "We don't play that shit here at ACU. We stand behind our message that everyone should feel safe and free to be themselves. I heard what folks have been saying about you. And let me just say, I'm sorry. I should've come to you sooner."

"Thank you." I was genuinely touched.

Outside of Alisha and maybe Dr. Collier, no one even acknowledged how I could be feeling. His words hit different, like finding someone on my side in a fight I never asked for. For the first time since that argument with Corey, I felt like I could take a full breath. The weight on my shoulders lightened, just enough for me to notice the difference. Not completely better, but something close to it.

"You just got here. You're a freshman. I get it. I know how that feels. You don't want to draw negative attention to yourself. We speak in general about bullying and harassment, but we can speak directly about you."

"No. No, please."

He paused and sighed. "Fine. We won't do anything you do not want us to do. Just know you are not alone, and we are here to support you." He touched my shoulder again and waited for me to respond.

"Thanks, Chris." I gave him a half smile.

"Alright, cool." He got up casually as if we had just been discussing homework for a class or what we were going to eat for dinner. He looked at his wristwatch and walked over to the orange, cloth-upholstered wingback chair.

"It's almost four o'clock. Please take your seats, and let's get this meeting started."

The door chimed again. My eyes darted in its direction. It was Alisha. Finally. My heart jumped a little when I saw her, like a basketball hovering on the rim, before deciding whether to fall in or roll off.

After days of silence between us, I had no idea where we stood or why she had suddenly disappeared. Her eyes swept across the room, pausing briefly but never looking in my direction. Her face gave nothing away, completely unreadable. She seemed liked her normal self.

Chapter Nine

She didn't even look at me when she walked in, but I knew she had to have seen me. A person couldn't walk through the door and not see me.

She sat in the only open seat behind Chris. He was so tall I couldn't make eye contact with her. Although I was looking directly at him the entire meeting, I barely listened to a word he said. I inconspicuously bobbed my head from right to left, trying to make eye contact with her, but it was no use.

"Alright, if no one has any other questions, let's break into our committees and get to work!" Chris clasped his hands together and stood, along with everyone else in the room, who chattered and moved around.

I got up to make my way over to Alisha, who was on her way out of the room.

"Hey, Chandon." Someone touched my arm, stopping me from following her out of the room. I turned around. Our committee's chairperson, Lisa, was smiling at me, her big, dark almond shaped eyes filled with excitement. Her heels made her seem taller than she was as she hovered over me in her light blue skirt suit.

"What's up?" I asked, my head turning toward Alisha's back as I watched her turn left down the hall toward where the *Loud and Proud* committee met. I turned back towards Lisa and forced a smile across my face.

"I've been looking for you around campus, but you been MIA! Matter of fact, I need your cell phone number so I can text you next time." She pulled out her cell phone.

"I'm excited to talk to you about how we should help build more of a social media following around Monica Jacobs and Lorraine Cuttleston. Like, we don't have a big enough presence on our social media platforms. We need something that's going to get people engaged and reposting. What you think?"

"Huh?" I turned in the direction Alisha had gone, then back toward Lisa. "I mean, yeah. Yeah, for sure."

She wrapped her arm around me. "Girl, come on. We got work to do!" She ushered me in the opposite direction of Alisha.

Fuck. I pulled out my phone to text Alisha.

What's up? I hit send.

Where have you been? Send.

I've been texting you. Send.

Are you okay? Send.

I rolled my eyes and sighed, the hot air rushing from my mouth with an exaggerated groan.

"What's up? You good?" I could feel Lisa's warm breath on my neck, smelling like spearmint. She hovered over me as we stood at the round table. The minty coolness lingered in the air between us, a stark contrast to the warmth of the room. The overhead lights caught the gold flecks in her dark eyes as she leaned closer. My hand clutched my phone. My eyes could have burned a hole in the screen.

"Lover's quarrel?" she smirked and nudged her elbow into mine.

I looked up, catching her staring at my screen, then back at me for a response. I shoved my phone in my back pocket.

"What? No!"

"Where's Alisha?"

I didn't reply; I just sat down in one of the chairs at the table and tapped my foot. Lisa sat in the chair next to me and pulled a notepad from her bookbag. She removed her suit jacket and wrapped it around the back of the chair. I could smell the light, flowery scent of her perfume. I watched her as she meticulously rolled up each of her sleeves.

"Unfortunately, Devin and Eleanor aren't going to make it today. They said they had some huge paper to write. Devin created several social media pages, and Eleanor created a change.org petition. There haven't been any posts created on the pages yet, though. The petition will be the first thing to go up. What do you think?"

I had pulled my phone out of my back pocket, turned away from her, and looked down at the empty space after my last sent messages to Alisha.

"Chandon?"

I placed my phone face down on the table.

"I'm sorry. What were you saying?"

"It's clear that you're distracted today, which isn't good since it's just me and you. I was hoping we could at least brainstorm some ideas for a plan of action around Monica Jacobs and Lorraine Cuttleston." She crossed her arms.

"I'm sorry."

"You said that already. What's going on? Why is Alisha in the other room? Has she joined *Loud & Proud*? I mean, that's fine, but a heads up would be nice."

"She hasn't—I mean, I don't know—she's not—" I stopped. I didn't know what the hell was going on with Alisha. "I don't have anything right now. I haven't even been focused on this."

Lisa rolled her eyes. "I know y'all are freshmen and this is still probably just a club to you, but we take things seriously around here when it comes to our community, supporting our

LGBTQ+ people, and being activists. That's who we are at ACU. A club of young activists.

"We're not just college students. That's our history, and that's why people join ACU. As you can see, it's not a lot of us, we're a small club compared to the others around campus, and we're okay with that. We aren't with people coming in here just to say they are a member of ACU.

"This is more than a social club." She paused. "It is young people like us," she pointed at her chest and then to me, "who start movements, Chandon."

"I know that."

"I'm not trying to lecture you. I'm trying to motivate you. It's clear that people see something in you that you don't see in yourself." She stood up and walked over to the desk, which was placed in the space that had once been a closet. She sat down at the leather office chair and turned on the computer.

"What do you mean, Lisa? People don't even know me. Yet everybody's got an opinion." I felt my jaw clench.

"Honestly, you're young, but you have strong leadership qualities. I like that about you," she said, her back towards me as she typed. She swiveled around and faced me.

"I was out there after Black Lives Matter came on campus. I saw Corey's messy ass start that fight with you in front of everybody, but you held your own. That had to feel crazy for you."

She paused. "And you had some valid points, by the way. I was excited when you joined this committee." She smiled.

"Th—thanks, Lisa. It hasn't been easy. Since that day, people been talking about me and saying some crazy shit. It hasn't been great," I confessed, dropping my shoulders.

"Fuck them!"

I gasped and did a double take at Lisa. I'd never heard her so much as raise her voice before. Her lips barely revealed a closed smile before her face was serious again.

"I'm serious. Don't let these people define you. You'll figure it out. In the meantime, I'm going to work on some stuff here by myself today. You can go, um, clear your mind? Figure out what's going on with you and your girl? I don't know, but next week, please be ready." She stared at me.

"What about a march to the Capitol?" My words came out unsteady. "Um…yeah, we—we'll march to the Capitol. We'll march to the Capitol from campus and—and have a protest right on its steps! That's it!" I surprised myself, but it felt right.

Maybe fighting for something bigger was part of the promise, too — even if I never spoke it out loud.

I sat up taller, my head lifted; my shoulders drawn back—like when I outwitted my grandfather in one of our debates. I could feel my heart begin to race.

She smiled widely. Picked up her note pad and began writing vigorously.

"I love it! Hell yeah." She shook her head. "We can see what local businesses in the community will help fundraise money by giving us a percentage from sales made by faculty and students at their stores. It'll increase business to their stores, a win-win."

I hopped from my seat over to Lisa and scooted a chair close to her. "Ooh, good idea. Has that ever been done before?" I asked.

"Oh, yeah. Businesses love participating in Franklin's fundraisers. That's one of the reasons I like it here, too, because people in the community tend to support our causes." She tapped her pencil's eraser on the notepad. "Hmm… How many miles is the Capitol from here? Is this march even realistic?"

I pulled out my phone. She touched my hand, our eyes locked.

"You're on a roll, girl. Don't look at your phone. I'll look it up here." She didn't wait for my response before she turned around, typing. Then she turned back to me, her cheekbones raised, her eyes glistening. She gave me two thumbs up.

"It's only a mile and a half away. Totally doable! Totally. Even with a large group of people walking slowly. It may take about an hour—but less than two, right?" She looked at me for confirmation.

I noticed she had the smallest black mole in the corner of her left nostril. For some reason, her excitement made me want to lean over and kiss her there. The sudden impulse caught me off guard. This had been happening a lot lately—Corey, Alisha, now Lisa?

Back home, there had only ever been Stephanie. Here at Franklin, it was like the floodgates had opened. These unexpected attractions pulling me in different directions, both exciting and confusing me all at once.

"Definitely." I smiled; my chin tilted up.

She pumped her fist. "Yes! We have a start. That's teamwork, Chandon." We fist-bumped each other.

There was a commotion from people talking and passing by our opened door. We both turned to look. I noticed Alisha walked by, headed toward the front door. My chin dropped to my chest as I released a deep, closed mouth exhale.

Just when I'd found my stride, there went Alisha, again. The moment of connection with Lisa fractured as my attention split between the excitement of our plans and the ache of whatever was happening with Alisha.

"It's cool," Lisa chuckled. "We at least have a starting point." She touched my arm. "Thank you for staying and being present." She shook her head. "That's what I'm talking about, what I can see about you. And other people can, too."

"Next week, I'm locked in," I said, the words rushing from me. My breathing grew heavier.

"Girl, bye." She chuckled and turned back towards the screen.

I hurried and grabbed my things, darting out the door. I walked out on the porch of Hester House just as Alisha headed down the last step.

"Lish, wait up." My voice revealed both desperation and confusion.

She turned, looked at me, and kept walking. I practically jumped off the steps after her.

"Hey, girl. Wait up. What happened? What's wrong?" I tried to keep up with her quickened pace.

It was a windy, cool evening. The sun had set, which made it feel cooler than I'd anticipated. All I had on was our school's embroidered sweatshirt; my backpack fastened tight on my shoulders. Alisha had on a red and black Chicago Bulls bomber jacket from the nineties, black jeans, and red and black Air Jordans. I really liked her style. Laid back but sexy. She fastened the buttons on her jacket.

"Lish," I pleaded.

She stopped abruptly. Her eyes looked dark and distant. "Don't 'Lish' me."

"What?"

"Nah, you don't get to do that. You don't get to act like some confused high school teenager. We're in college now, and I don't have time for this—for you." She kept walking.

"Wait a minute, Lish." I reached for her arm. She turned around quickly, her hot breath warming my chilled cheeks. Her chest heaving, almost touching mine. Her finger pointed at my forehead. My eyes widened and froze.

"Don't put your hands on me, Chandon. Don't touch me." She clenched her teeth.

I stepped back in shock. My hand stung, not from her touch but from the rejection; the space between us suddenly charged with something I couldn't name.

The wind whipped through the branches causing gold, brown, red, and yellow crispy leaves to fall from the huge maple tree we stood under. Pulled by the crisp air, they danced like tap shoes down the street. The streetlight was dim, but I could see the anger in Alisha's eyes. They illuminated the space between us clearly and burned brighter than any streetlight could.

"I didn't mean to—I—"

"Just because you didn't mean to doesn't mean it didn't happen. You can't just touch me whenever you want to."

"Y—you're right. You're right. I'm sorry. I wasn't trying to hurt you."

"Well…you did." She folded her arms.

"Come on, Lish, I barely touched your arm."

"I'm not talking about my fucking arm, Chandon. You really *are* from Willowbrook, huh?" She shook her head.

The way she said "Willowbrook" cut deeper than I expected, like she was using my city as evidence of some flaw in who I was.

"Yeah! Yeah, I am." I threw my arms in the arm. "So what?" I was fed up with the accusations and judgements from folks about who I was.

"So what? You're clueless! The other day in the hallway—" She stared at me for confirmation.

I frowned. "What about it?"

She exhaled and started walking again. I moved with a light jog to keep up with her long, quick strides.

"Did I say something wrong? What? What did I say?" I pleaded in between breaths.

"You good, Chandon." She smirked and shook her head in disbelief.

I stopped, my feet planted firmly on the gray concrete alongside the treelined street, with luxury and foreign cars parked on its curb. Most of them driven by our professors who chose to live close to campus. The windows glowed from many of the homes we passed like the tail ends of lighting bugs in the summer.

"Tell me, dammit!" I demanded.

She stopped and turned to me. Her eyes flickered. She looked me up and down.

"Mmph, okay." She walked over to where I stood. "Every time that girl—*Corey*—shows up, you act like you don't know me. Like I barely exist to you."

She said Corey's name as if she weren't sure it was her name. It came out of her mouth in a drawl, like it was hard for her to say. "That's not cool." Her eyes seemed to soften with her tone.

"I don't appreciate that. I thought we—I mean," she sighed, "if we're friends, treat me like it. You said you'd meet me outside, so I waited for you."

The moment flashed through my mind like a movie on fast forward. The hallway. Corey walking up. Me turning away from Alisha mid-sentence, like she had suddenly become invisible. The hurt in her eyes that I'd chosen not to see. *Fuck!*

"I apologize. You're right. You have been my only friend around here and I don't want you to think I take that—*you*—for granted."

Her head tilted to the side, inspecting me curiously. Her lips parted; I waited for her to speak. She took a deep breath, grabbed the straps on her backpack, and leaned her weight to one side.

"*Friends?* You sure that's what we are?" A single eyebrow raised. We stared at each other.

I felt a rush of warm energy like warm cocoa move from my belly, where it tap danced like the leaves, moving on down to the center of my thighs and beginning to tingle there. The sensation spread outward, giving me chills that prickled up my arms and hardened my nipples. My body caught between the inner heat and the cool fall air wrapping around us.

"I—I'm your friend." I swallowed, the word feeling like a half-truth.

"Okay, *friend*." Her lips pursed, the emphasis carrying all her disappointment. For a moment, her eyes searched mine, looking for something more honest than what I was offering. "Just don't keep disappearing on me every time *someone else* shows up."

"I hear you, Lish. And I won't do that again. I really missed you."

She linked her arm into mine, which made me feel warm like cocoa again. "I missed you, too!"

We laughed in relief and bounced arm-in-arm toward the yard.

"So, what happened in committee today?"

"Oooh, I'm so excited to tell you about that! You are coming back, right?" I gave her a sideways glance.

She smiled. "Yeah, I'll be back."

Chapter Ten

"We need to focus on messaging first," I said, surprising myself with how confident my voice sounded.

I sat with the others around the table in the Marsha P. Johnson room. They stared at me with new interest. Even Devin, who'd missed last week's meeting, leaned forward slightly. I felt Alisha's foot nudge mine under the table, a subtle signal of support. This wasn't like my first few committee meetings, where I'd felt like an imposter. Now, I was driving the conversation, and it felt right.

"We need to be clear about what we're asking for, specifically about Monica Jacobs and Lorraine Cuttleston. Then we can build the logistics around that message," I continued.

All eyes in the room were on me. Just weeks ago, this spotlight would have sent me retreating into silence. But something had shifted since my argument with Corey, since Dr. Collier's push, and since reconciling with Alisha.

The weight of others' expectations, my grandfather's, my mother's, even Corey's, had forced me to carefully calculate what to say. But here, in this moment, I wasn't calculating. I was just speaking.

"Exactly," Alisha chimed in, leaning forward. "And we need to think about how to get more student organizations involved. The more diverse the participation, the more attention we'll get. The more attention we get, the more powerful our protest becomes."

"I love how you two are thinking about this," Lisa nodded approvingly. "Let's break it down step by step. We also need permits, a clear route, safety protocols..."

Lisa spread a city map across the table like a general preparing for battle. The paper rustled as she smoothed it flat, the creases creating valleys and ridges beneath her fingertips. The faint scent of her flowery perfume cut through the musty perfume of history that hung in the air of Hester House. A blend of old books, wood polish, and the lingering whispers of past activists who'd once gathered in these same rooms.

I traced the path from Franklin to the Capitol with my finger, feeling an electric current race up my arm. This wasn't just a line on a map; it was a declaration. Our footsteps would beat a rhythm of protest against the concrete, demanding to be heard. I could feel the pride and confidence swell up inside of me, I wasn't just participating I was creating something that mattered.

Devin was locked in and focused. Eleanor had already started taking notes, her pen poised above her notebook. They weren't just humoring me, they were taking me seriously. The realization straightened my spine.

As the day went on, we went back and forth about what message we wanted to get across. We continued outlining the practical concerns. I caught Devin and Eleanor exchanging impressed glances. This wasn't just an idea anymore. It was becoming real, becoming mine in a way I hadn't expected.

All those debates with my grandfather, where he'd trapped me in arguments about history, philosophy, race, and politics, had prepared me for something after all. But this felt different. This wasn't about pleasing him or proving myself to him. This was something I actually wanted to do.

Monica and Lorraine's imprisonment resonated with me; their identities questioned and policed. Different circumstances but that feeling of never quite belonging anywhere? That, I understood all too well.

And there was something deep in my heart pulling me toward this cause—my dad. The weight of his dog tags against my chest reminded me of his sacrifice, his dedication to his country, and to us. I couldn't help thinking that if my dad were here, he would stand up for his fellow soldiers without hesitation.

For once, I wasn't just debating theory with my grandfather. I was putting his lessons into practice. And I wasn't reacting to what anyone else wanted me to be. I wanted to make myself proud.

Chapter Eleven

It was the Friday before fall break, and Asher was about to arrive for a visit. I had gotten so caught up in ACU that I'd stopped counting down the days.

I was amazed at how many people didn't know about Monica Jacobs and Lorraine Cuttleston. It was sad, too. How could two US veterans be held captive in another country and it not be national news? How could there not be protests? And barbershop and beauty salon conversations?

Yet, when we went into the shops, a lot of us students frequented for haircuts and hairdos; the people inside sounded like a wilderness packed full of owls when we asked them about the two women. *Who* was always the first question?

The lack of awareness and coverage of their situation energized me, Alisha, Lisa, Devin, and Eleanor. The bogus charges were really a front for the fact that they were gay in a country where being gay was unlawful. The case was serious. The women could spend up to twenty years in a Kuwaiti prison.

Before I left my dorm room each morning, every time we passed out flyers or walked through the community, I kissed my dad's dog tags and whispered a thank you. For his protection. For his guidance. The ache in my chest was so strong some days, I had no choice but to call my mom, just to feel a little closer to him.

"Your father would be so proud, Donny. I know I am. I'm so happy you're liking it there. I was a little worried," she admitted. That was the first time I heard her confess any reservations about me coming to Franklin.

"You were?" I asked.

"Of course. You've never been away from home more than a couple of weeks at a time and—just a mother's worries, that's all."

"Oh," was all I said. "I been thinking about dad even more since I been working on this protest at the Capitol."

"I wish I could give you a hug." I noticed she didn't say she missed him, too, which was also a first.

"I had a dream about him the other night. In the dream, he dropped me off here at Franklin. I don't know where we were coming from. But it was weird because when I was getting out of his car—which was some type of military vehicle—he said, 'Keep going, baby girl.'" I sniffled.

"He's always going to be with you, Donny," she assured me in a calming tone that I needed to hear.

"With us," I corrected.

"Yeah. Um—hold on. Your brother is pulling at my arm like it's not attached."

Then, my brother's voice came through. Only I could hardly recognize the deep, raspy tone. "E.J?"

He gave a slight chuckle. "Yeah."

"Oh, boy. I bet you think you're something now!" I chuckled.

"Well, you know. The voice is attracting the ladies."

"Oh, God. Please stop it."

"I've been texting you. You are not that busy."

"Yes, I am. Now, what do you want?" I asked in my annoyed big sister tone. But I really missed him.

"I was trying to come there for your fall break since you ditched us and didn't want to come home. I thought your lame ass—"

I heard my mom in the background telling him to watch his language.

"Sorry, mom," he apologized, then whispered, "I thought your lame ass wasn't going to make any friends!" He chuckled. "Not without Asher."

"For your information, I am doing just fine."

"Then let me come!" Even with his new deep voice, he still whined like my little baby brother.

"Soon. Anyway, I thought you'd be happy having the house free of me." I teased.

"Well, for *your* information." I heard the creaking sound of a door open, then close. He lowered his voice. "The house isn't exactly empty. Mom is dating some lame-ass dude named Carl."

"What?"

"Yeah, and I need to get out of here. It's weird."

I felt my heart sink into my stomach and then felt it begin to beat rapidly. I was already on my bed, so I laid down, put my hand on my head and began to massage my temple. I took a few slow and quiet deep breaths.

"Um, you there? Say something!"

"What is there to say, EJ? I don't even know what to do with this information."

"Shit. Me either. That's why I've been trying to call you; she gave no warning. One day, I came home to dinner with this tall lumberjack-looking dude sitting at the table, smiling at me like we knew each other. Motherfucker was trying too hard from the jump."

"He's—he's White?" I asked. Then added, "not that it matters."

"Yeah, I said *lumberjack*. What is Franklin teaching you," he sighed.

My stomach tightened at the image. My mom dating a White guy? I'd never even seen her look twice at anyone since Dad died, and now she was bringing home some bearded White dude to meet my brother. I couldn't decide what bothered me more, that she was dating at all or that she hadn't bothered to tell me. Then, I thought about how my grandfather would react when he inevitably found out. No doubt the explosion would be nuclear.

"He's not—not living there, is he?" I could barely fix my lips to ask the question.

"Hell no. I'm not having that."

I smiled at his protective tone. "Good." I paused and gathered myself. I realized he needed my reassurance. "Look, mom is—well, she must trust him to bring him around you. We haven't seen mom date a single person since—maybe give him a chance."

His response was an exaggerated, open-mouthed exhale.

"Okay? Get to know him…and report back to me with your findings," I added, giving him a mission.

Since he was a kid, anytime we needed him to get anything done, we'd send him on a private mission. He loved the idea of pretending to do what Dad had done when he was alive, even if they'd never met.

"Fine, but you owe me."

When I hung up, I felt more stressed and worried than I had before I called. *See, this is why I don't call home*, I thought.

I decided to take a walk around the yard. The majestic energy of the campus calmed my nerves and brought me peace. The tall trees with their huge trunks seemed to hold many stories, all their own. Sometimes, I'd quietly ask them to tell me one as I sat. Imagining myself listening to the stories, slowed my heart and racing mind. It helped me to focus.

The campus was quiet. A lot of students were either gone or packing up to leave for the week. The usual bustle had given way to an eerie calm that made even the sounds of my footsteps seem louder against the brick pathways. The air felt different, too, cleaner somehow, as if even the atmosphere was taking a break from the usual academic pressure. Squirrels felt it, too. They raced across the leaf-covered grass, scurrying back up tree trunks and disappearing into holes. I looked forward to the break, too. Plus, I would have Asher to myself all week, and that's all I needed.

I chose a tree that I'd never sat by before. Its trunk was wide, and its above-ground roots sprawled across the grass like a spider's legs. The black metal bench I sat on gave me a view of Nash-Jamison Hall all the way at the front of the campus as well as three other buildings, including our chapel with its tall pointed domed structure.

I remember my grandfather telling me that inside the chapel sat one of the rarest organs in the world, its value exceeding two million dollars. It was the only reason I went to church soon after I arrived on campus. I wanted to hear and see, in person, an instrument worth that much money. It did permeate the pews and make everyone jump to their feet, clap their hands, and raise their hands to the heavens, but in a conservative and dignified kind of way.

The service was somewhere in the middle of both of my family's churches back home—my mom's side, all hushed reverence and piano hymns, and my dad's side, where the choir stomped, shouted, and sometimes caught the Holy Ghost.

The sound each key made drew me into the choir's melodies as I sang along, but not enough for me to make a habit of attending regularly.

I sat and watched as birds chirped and flew over my head. They rested on building rooftops and hopped around in the grass before they took flight again. I was in the perfect place to get lost in thought. The wind was calm, but it was still a brisk fall day.

I had on my oversized dark blue sweater jacket, my favorite pair of jeans, and tight-knit cream turtleneck. I felt cute with my hair pulled up into a messy bun. My brown leather, worn-in ankle boots with a slight heel completed the look. The leather was soft but still held the shape of every step I'd ever taken, creasing at the toes in familiar folds. Cute and comfortable, I thought, when I looked at myself in the full-length mirror that morning.

I thought about texting Asher to confirm his arrival tomorrow. I thought about texting Lisa to see if she'd made up her mind about staying on campus for the week or going home. I even considered hitting up Ebony and Tashia from Dr. Collier's class about that kickback they'd mentioned.

We'd gone from those tense classroom arguments to grabbing lunch together occasionally, Ebony's sharp wit making her hilarious once she wasn't directing it at me, and Tashia knowing every underground event happening on or near campus. It still surprised me sometimes—how people who'd once seemed like opponents had become something like friends.

It took three meetings before a majority of votes approved the name for our protest: Operation Protect Those Who Protect Us. We were determined to do everything we could to bring Monica Jacobs and Lorraine Cuttleston home. The name felt powerful. They fought to protect us, and now we would fight to protect them.

We were all excited about our progress. But the down time away from all the planning would be great for everyone. I really hadn't had much time to kick back and chill or party like most first-year college students who were away from home for the first time.

My grandfather called weekly, like clockwork, to remind me that I wasn't at Franklin for the academics alone, but to grow into a leader. Blah. Blah. Blah. I thought. Why couldn't he just ask me how I was coming along?

"We are a family dedicated to serving others," he'd lecture me. I'd be rolling my eyes so hard they could have rolled out the back of my head, but since I'd joined ACU, I was becoming more comfortable with the idea that I was a leader. The more I worked to put together *Protect Those Who Protect Us* protest, the more I enjoyed the urgency of creating change.

My thoughts were interrupted because within my line of vision, about one hundred yards away, was the front entrance of Ella Baker Hall, our admissions office building.

Baker Hall looked more like a modern-day castle than a university building, with its square three-tiered tower. The long path leading up to its arched wooden double doors made it feel even more castle-like. It was magical and gave me a tingling feeling all over.

I remember walking the path with my grandfather and mom during a visit. The building itself made me feel small and a little unworthy.

It wasn't the building that caught my attention, though. I leaned forward and squinted my eyes, trying to focus on a tall, lanky figure in the distance. There was something familiar about his movements, the way he held himself while checking his phone.

A strange flutter of recognition hit me. That couldn't be... I shook my head, trying to clear it. God, I missed Asher more than I thought if I was seeing him in random strangers. I chuckled at myself but found my gaze drawn back to the figure.

Looking closer, I realized the resemblance was uncanny. Same warm brown skin tone, same straight-out-of-J. Crew style that somehow never looked pretentious on him. When he turned his face toward me, the sun caught the edge of his black-rimmed glasses, and my heart leapt.

"No way," I whispered, already rising to my feet.

As I moved closer, my uncertainty gave way. My pace quickened with each step until I was running full-out across the yard, a scream of surprise and joy escaping me as I bolted toward my best friend.

"Asher!" When I reached him, I almost jumped into his arms. He was laughing and hugging me back.

"Girl, stop acting like we long lost pals," he teased.

"Dude, you told me you weren't coming until tomorrow! What are you doing here?" I wiped happy tears from my eyes.

"You must've really missed me." He smiled.

"Seriously, why didn't you tell me you were here?" I asked, my hands on my hips.

His shoulders slumped as he sighed. "I don't know, Don. I don't know. I hate it there, so I came over here to talk to an advisor." He gave me *don't hate me* eyes. "I didn't want anybody talking me out of it, so I didn't tell anyone."

"Not even me?" I asked, my hand gripping my chest.

"It's not like that, Don. I just had to do this one on my own."

"Okay, I guess." I looked around. "Uh, where are your bags, then?"

"Um…" he hesitated. Then his gaze fixed on something behind me.

I turned around. My stomach fluttered, and my mouth dropped.

"Asher Johnson? Are you ready for your tour?" Corey walked up casually.

She looked nothing like the sloppy-looking, carefree geek I'd met at the elevator. She had on a pair of black kiltie leather loafers, no socks. Her black creased slacks stopped right at her ankle like they were tailored.

Her crispy white collared shirt was tucked in, unbuttoned right before it reached her cleavage. Her eyeglass arms were still adorned with tape, but her Afro was perfectly blown out and evenly round, and her glossed lips looked soft and kissable.

Suddenly, the sweater jacket I had on made me feel hot instead of warm and cozy. I felt the sweat building underneath my breasts. I wanted to cross my legs to quell the pulsating urge that began to thump at the sight of her looking so dapper.

I was so aroused I could feel it in my panties and grew concerned it would betray me through my denim jeans. She didn't even acknowledge me.

"What the fuck?" I managed.

"Don, I'm sorry. I was hoping I could get through the tour without running into you," Asher said.

"Running into me?" My mind struggled to process Asher's words and Corey's updated look. It was all coming at me too fast. The crisp white shirt, the perfectly tailored pants, even the deliberate confidence in the way she stood. This was a Corey I hadn't seen before, and my brain was short-circuiting trying to reconcile this image with the person who'd pressed me from the moment I met her in the elevator wearing dirty Chucks and a Don King-like Afro.

"I was gonna call you right after."

"Tour?" My mouth still hung open.

"Yeah." Corey licked her lips. "I'm here to show Asher around Franklin. Do y'all know each other?" She looked between us.

"Yes, we do. Is it okay if she joins us? I didn't tell Dean Saunders I knew anyone here because I'm really trying to do this on my own. What's your name?" Asher reached out to shake Corey's hand.

My emotions were a tangled mess. First, a moment of relief that Asher asked if I could stay. Then, confusion about why he hadn't told me about this tour in the first place, and a strange possessiveness I couldn't quite name.

Was I jealous that Corey was showing him around? That he might transfer here without me being part of the decision? Or was I just thrown off balance seeing these two parts of my life collide without warning?

Whatever it was, it left me feeling like I was somehow both essential and irrelevant to this moment.

A smile spread across Corey's face. "Corey," she said, slow and deliberate, as if she knew for sure he'd heard it before.

Asher's eyes widened until I could see more white than brown in them. After they shook hands, he put his hands in his pockets and swayed from side to side. He sucked his lips into his mouth as if it was the only way to keep him from talking. One of the first times he'd been speechless, I thought.

"Ya girl can come if she wants to," Corey said. She lifted the sleeve on her blazer, which revealed her silver chronograph watch. "All I know is I promised the Dean a one-hour tour. So, let's do it." Corey's mischievous smile told me all I needed to know.

"Corey," Asher said, "I hope the men here are as fine as you are, honey, because you are gorgeous!"

"Personally, I wouldn't know. But today's not the best day to find out since most folks will be going back home, or to Cancun, or to wherever."

"What about you? Are you headed home after this?"

"Nah, not me. I'll be right here." She looked at Asher. "Small world, though, huh?"

"For sure." Asher glanced back at me.

"We'll start at our library, which is named after Malcolm X and Betty Shabazz." Her voice changed from comfortable and casual to all business.

I was all business, too. My eyes were locked in on her round, tight ass; it formed a perfectly firm peach shape against her pant slacks. I'd never gotten to see any parts of her figure through the oversized clothes she usually wore. My body tingled and perspired with excitement.

I trailed slightly behind them as we made our way around campus, feeling increasingly like an afterthought in what should have been my reunion with Asher. Yes, I was still distracted by how good Corey looked in that outfit, the tailored pants showcasing a figure I'd never gotten to see. But that attraction was mixed with growing irritation. This wasn't how I'd planned to spend time with my best friend.

The rest of the tour blended together as Corey guided us through campus. Losing her usual intense demeanor, she moved with ease between buildings, the library, the science building, and the art galleries. She even pointed out hidden study spots.

I found myself crossing my arms, checking my phone, and fighting the urge to interrupt with, 'I could have shown you that,' every time Corey pointed out something I already knew.

Each time Asher nodded enthusiastically at her explanations, each question he asked that he'd never bothered to ask me about my own college experience, I felt even more sidelined.

What struck me most was how animated Corey became when talking about tradition and legacy, how different she seemed from the confrontational activist who'd challenged me on the yard. Asher somehow managed to draw out this side of her, and they fell into a rhythm that left me trailing slightly behind, unsure whether to feel annoyed or intrigued at how quickly they'd connected.

What was even happening? Asher was here a day early, hadn't told me he was coming, and now I was tagging along on a tour of my own damn campus while my best friend and my...whatever Corey was, acted like they'd known each other for years.

Was I more upset that he was considering transferring to Franklin without telling me or that he seemed to have an instant connection with Corey that I hadn't been able to achieve.

She shared stories about Franklin's history with obvious pride. Most of them I'd already heard, but I understood exactly what she meant when she said she felt like Franklin chose her. From the moment I stepped foot on the campus, I knew I belonged here, too. It was just a feeling that came over me.

Seeing all the Black students coming and going in all types of attire, from suits and ties to dresses, skirts, and heels, all the way down to joggers and slides; I hadn't seen anything like it before. And I could imagine myself being among them.

The professors I met and the aura and vibe of the campus, surrounded by beautiful trees and an immaculately kept yard, re-inforced that feeling. The buildings stood tall with pride, like a fortress of protection. I felt welcomed and safe.

Asher spoke to Corey freely, as if they'd known each other before this tour. He said he'd wanted to go to Franklin from the beginning but felt the pressure from his dad to attend an Ivy League school. He applied and got into Franklin, but his dad said he wouldn't support him financially if he attended. Why didn't I know these things, and why was he sharing them with *her?*

I was used to Asher making fast friends with others, but this was weird because I'd talked to him about Corey. He knew how I felt about her. He was supposed to be on my side, not chumming it up with her.

Nash-Jamison Hall was our final stop. Corey paused at the top of the steps and looked out over the campus, her eyes unblinking and focused. Something in her expression shifted—a darkness falling over her features that seemed to come from nowhere.

But then I remembered Chris's words from our conversation at Hester House: "She has a deeper story—a tragedy, really. A trauma that blazes her passion and doesn't allow her to see widely enough."

The memory sent a chill through me as Corey's eyes remained fixed on some distant point, her body suddenly still. I glanced at Asher, who looked back at me with slight confusion, both of us sensing the abrupt change in atmosphere.

"Twelve years ago, my cousins and I were playing on the front stoop of our house, right on the steps. It was hot, muggy, and humid; it was July on the East Coast, you know? We were waiting for my uncle Lonny to get home so we'd be allowed to ride our bikes.

"We always played on the front stoop because my auntie didn't let us do much else. She was strict like that. We were sitting there arguing over basketball cards and shit: which card was better or worth the most, you know?" Corey's eyes looked toward the sky.

"My uncle drove this super clean, dope-ass dark blue Chevy Monte Carlo. It was so shiny you could see yourself in the glossy paint. He loved that car, man." She shook her head.

"It had shiny silver rims and tinted windows. Clean. It smelled so clean when you got inside. He never smoked with the windows up. Never. He never let us eat in it either—not even drink water. She chuckled.

"He had a routine, you know? So, when he pulled up, he had his music playing like always. Uncle Lonny had the loudest car speakers on the block, man. He'd open his trunk, and we'd all be jamming to Earth, Wind, & Fire, or James Brown, or some old-school joint because that's what he liked to bump.

"He told us we didn't know nothing about music. So, he pulled up and parked in his usual spot on the curb right in front of our red-bricked row house they owned. We all excited because we just knew we were about to get our bikes out and ride to the park.

"He rolled down his windows, then lit his cigarette. Same routine every day. Except this time, a cop car pulled up alongside his car. We don't even notice it at first.

"We are not really paying too much attention because we already know what he is doing because he does the same thing every day. And my cousin LJ is trippin' because he really thought his Dominique Wilkins card was worth more than my Magic Johnson card. I mean, we were going at it, too.

"Before we knew it, the next time we looked up, the cops were out of their car with their nine-millimeter black, heavy metal guns quivering in their pale hands, pointed right at my uncle while he sat in his car smoking his cigarette.

"They shouted at him to get out of the car. Their voices permeated my eardrums so deeply that I can still hear the hate and fear in their coward voices. I can still see the spit flying from their pink lips. Their red cheeks boiling with fear and anger."

'Get out of the car!'

"They just kept yelling it over and over. I can see my uncle frozen. He is shaking. His whole body is shaking. We can hear him when he finally speaks because none of us made a sound. He was chilling, you know? Smoking his cigarette, listening to Donny Hathaway's *Someday We'll All Be Free.*

'OK, officers, no p-problem. I live right here. Let me unbuckle my—my seatbelt.'

"His cigarette not even in his mouth no more. One of the cop's hands was shaking so bad, like the ground underneath his feet was moving.

'Get out of the fucking car…slowly, motherfucker! Slowly!'

"That's what the cop closest to him yelled again.

'Get out of the car or we're going to blow your fucking head off.'

"Me and my cousins are standing up now. We froze like we were on the TV screen, and someone had hit pause on us. We not even breathing. Scared to move. Scared to talk. Scared to watch. Scared not to watch. My uncle reached…he reached, slowly, too. He slowly reached to unbuckle his seatbelt, you know, like they told him to do, right?"

Corey's hand motioned by her hip as if she was unfastening her seat belt. The tears in her eyes threatened to fall as she continued to look toward the sky. "As soon as he unclicked his seatbelt, the cop closest to my uncle screamed out that bullshit.

'He's got a gun!'

"The shots rang out like a line of powerful firecrackers on the fourth of July. That's what it sounded like to me. Fireworks. Just a never-ending barrage of bullets at one Black man sitting in his car smoking a cigarette after work in front of his house, where his kids and niece sat and watched in utter horror and disbelief." Corey's face was wet with tears.

"He still had on his work shirt. Name tag stitched on his light blue mechanic's shirt. Red trimmed, white patch; *Londale* stitched in black. Murdered. In front of his two kids and niece. A niece he and his wife adopted when she was still a baby. The only father I ever knew…Uncle Lonny. Because he *fit the description*. The description of what? A Black husband, father, uncle. Gone. The end."

I looked at Asher. His face was wet with tears, too. Asher stared back at me. I touched my own damp face and wiped away the tears.

"It was on these steps that I heard my uncle Lonny's voice tell me I had found the right school. And if you stand here and hear a whisper, it's your ancestors. If you feel it resonates with you right here, Asher—" she turned and looked at him and touched her heart "—right here. Then maybe you've found the right school, too."

We stood in silence for a long while. As Corey's words hung in the air, I found myself seeing her differently. This wasn't just the confrontational activist who'd embarrassed me on the yard or even the polished student ambassador who'd been showing us around.

Corey had witnessed unspeakable trauma and somehow channeled it into purpose. Even the campus around us seemed quieter as if acknowledging the weight of what we'd just heard.

"I didn't mean to bring down the mood." She paused. Then, suddenly shifted back into tour guide mode. "Well, that concludes your official tour."

With a glance at her watch, she added, "Actually, I'm way beyond my scheduled hour with you. Let's go get some southern comfort food before the café closes!" She brushed her tears away with her hands, wiped them on her slacks, and headed down the steps.

In the café, a few small groups of students sat at the dining tables eating and talking, stuck on campus with no way home. Or, like me, with no real desire to go home.

I chose a chicken salad from The Burger Den and sat at one of the bar stool tables for two next to the windows. I hoped Corey would get the hint now that the tour was done and give me some time alone with Asher.

"Girl, how can you be eating salad with all this delicious food to choose from?" he said when he joined me. He smiled from ear to ear with excitement. His tray was filled with banana pudding, mac and cheese, greens, and fried chicken.

"It gets old fast."

"Why are we sitting at this two-seater? Where is Corey supposed to sit?" He looked around.

"Oh, so you team Corey, now?"

"What? Don, stop it. She's my tour guide. Besides, I can see why you're enamored by her." He smiled wide.

Corey walked up just then and put her tray in the small space between ours, grabbing a bar stool from another table and pulling it up to ours. The rest of lunch passed in a blur of casual conversation. Corey referred to me as 'Freshy' again.

Asher burst into laughter.

"I'm sorry," she sighed. "I'm sorry. Chandon."

"Why is it so hard to call me by my name, huh?"

I watched as Corey and Asher continued to connect like old friends while I floated somewhere above it all. When we finally finished eating, Asher stretched and checked his phone.

"I should probably get my stuff to your room and unpack," he said, gathering his tray.

"I can walk with you guys back to the dorms," Corey offered her eyes briefly meeting mine. "If that's okay?"

I couldn't think of a reason to say no that wouldn't sound rude, so I just nodded, unsure how to feel about extending this unexpected threesome any longer. As we approached my dorm building, I noticed Corey hang back slightly.

"Uh—hey, Chandon, can I speak to you for a sec, please?" Her voice was unusually low and unsteady.

I looked at Asher, who tried not to smile but already had his hand out for my key card.

"I got it. What's your room number?" He picked up his bags, opened the door, placed a bag there to prop it open, handed me my card back, and disappeared inside.

With just Corey and me there, my heart sped up, and the butterflies returned to their play inside of my belly.

"From the moment I saw you getting on that elevator, I wanted to get to know you. I just—you being a freshman, don't even matter to me. That's not why I call you Freshy." Her eyes wandered over my body and warmed me from the inside. "You're a breath of fresh air for me."

My mouth opened, but no words came out.

"Chandon, I hope you would be willing to give me a chance to—to… give me a chance to show you that I'm interested in you beyond what club you join or don't join. Or your thoughts on Black Lives Matter or who you're voting for." She stepped back.

"I'm not saying we won't argue or disagree about that stuff, 'cause my purpose won't change for no one. But I can tell you're so much more than that. And—"

I was on the fluffiest cotton ball cloud in the sky. It floated me right over to her. We stood there for a moment, looking at each other. Her eyes danced with emotion as they searched mine.

The silence between us loud. I thought about all our interactions, meeting her in the elevator to the confrontation on the yard, her visit to my dorm room, then colliding in the hallway, and the cool distance we'd maintained during most of the tour.

I thought about Chris's words about her trauma, about the raw pain in her voice when she'd told us about her uncle. There were so many layers to Corey I was only beginning to see, like looking at a painting up close and suddenly stepping back to see the full image.

For weeks, I'd been fighting whatever this was—these feelings that kept popping up with Corey, with Alisha, and even with Lisa during committee meetings. I didn't care anymore. I wasn't overthinking who I was supposed to be or what anybody would think. For once, I was just going with what felt right.

I held her hands in mine, embraced my racing heart, then closed my eyes. The electricity of our lips joined together and the friction of our bodies grazing against each other's, sent Niagara Falls cascading from the crown of my head to the center of my body, where my thighs separated but still functioned together as one.

There, the excitement of the moment danced around my button, and the intensity of the pressure almost caused me to explode. When our lips parted, we shared no words.

I entered my building, the door closed behind me, and I exhaled and released those happy butterflies and watched them fly all around me. I heard Corey's release, too. An emphatic scream of *YES!* from the other side of the door. I drifted up the stairs to meet Asher.

When I opened my door, Asher stood there waiting.

"Sooo?" His eyebrows lifted expectantly.

"I kissed her!" I whispered, then fell back on my bed, clutching my heart.

"I knew it! Girrrrl…*and?*"

"It was… perfect!"

He pulled me up from the bed, and we jumped around, hands clasped, as if we'd just won a Publisher's Clearinghouse sweepstake. I couldn't stop smiling. My phone buzzed with a text from Corey.

Hey, Freshy. I can still feel your lips on mine.

Asher read it over my shoulder and fanned himself dramatically. "Girl, you've got an upperclassman who is clearly into you. That's hot!"

I laughed as he pretended to ward off invisible heat waves coming from my body.

"You're crazy," I said, shaking my head at my friend but feeling my cheeks flush warm.

Chapter Twelve

The next day, I took Asher with me to Hester House. I was excited to show him around and see what he thought about our protest plans. Even dressed casually, Asher looked J. Crew clean.

He wore a light gray jogger set with three shirts layered underneath the unzipped hooded jacket. The first was white, the second was red, and the last had blue and white vertical stripes. His sleeves were scrunched up, and he matched it with a pair of black and gray high-top Nike Blazers.

I'd already taken him through the house, and now we were seated at the round table in Marsha P. Johnson's room, looking at the plans we had solidified for the protest. When I'd first shown him the photos of the activists on the walls, he'd gone quiet, studying their faces with an intensity I rarely saw from him.

"They look so... determined," he'd finally said. "Like they knew exactly what they were fighting for." It was strange seeing my normally chatty friend speechless, his fingers tracing the edges of a newspaper clipping about Franklin's first Pride celebration on the yard.

"This campus is just so amazing! This house, this room, it's just so—it makes me feel like it was meant for me to be here, you know?"

I shook my head and smiled. I knew how he felt.

"Once I transfer, I think I'll probably become a member, too," he said with a hint of mischief in his voice.

"What?" I whipped my head towards him.

"Girl, you should see your face right now!" He burst into laughter. "I'm just playing with you. Can you imagine *me* planning protests and making signs? This is *your* thing, not mine."

"But you just said—"

"I'm not saying it's not impressive," he backpedaled, gesturing to the room. "It's just—you know me. I'm more of a behind-the-scenes supporter. I'll help you pass out flyers and stuff, but I don't think I'm cut out for the frontlines like you." He sarcastically raised a closed fist into the air.

"I know, not me, right?" I mimicked him. "But just—thinking about my dad, I just—"

He looked away from me, the joke suddenly fading from his face.

"Well, you never know...if you can change your mind, maybe I'll change mine, too!" he snapped.

"How did I—"

"Oh, bitch, no!" he jumped up and started switching around the room, impersonating my walk and talk. "'Cause everybody ain't gon be marching in the street, Asher.'"

"True. True. I did say that." I shook my head and laughed. "But now that I'm actually up close and personal with how protesting and marching changed shit right here on this campus not even that long ago, I'm thinking differently about it. I mean, it's why we're standing in this house right now." I pointed down at the dark wooden floors.

"I don't know, I just wanna—wanna see if maybe we can do the same. I mean look at this, Ash. Look at what they accomplished."

I watched as his eyes roamed across the wall at the posters, some in black & white, most in color: images of LGBTQ+ leaders and student activists frozen in time, marching with fists in the air, eyes focused and determined, mouths open wide, with chants and demands for freedom and equality.

There were even some framed newspaper clippings, large framed bold, black-lettered inspirational quotes, and photos of students who stood on the steps in front of Nash-Jamison Hall with bullhorns at their mouths, speaking out to a crowd of their peers.

The images were so powerful to me that every time I came into the house, I was compelled to look at them and imagine what it must have felt like for the students to organize and create the type of change they were able to accomplish. I envisioned us one day being frozen in action on the wall, too.

"And honestly, if it wasn't for this group—this space, I don't even know…would I even still be here at this school?"

I turned from my thoughts to feel Asher's eyes on me. He smiled at me, and I smiled back.

"What?" I asked, seeing the odd look he had on his face.

"Nothing, it's just that—" he pretended to sniffle and wipe away invisible tears— "I'm just so proud of you!"

"You're silly." I blushed. "Thanks, though. But I'm not doing this alone. We're a small but mighty group. I think they all went home for the week, though."

"So why the hell are we in here working?" he looked around.

"Oh, come on! It's only for a little bit, and I swear we'll go do something fun."

"I'm glad you realize this ain't fun," he pretended to mumble.

"What's that?" I leaned my ear closer as if I hadn't heard his snarky comment.

"I knew it was you in here when I saw the light on. Girl, take a break!" Alisha said, leaned up against the entryway.

Asher and I both turned quick.

"Girl," I clutched my chest. "We did not hear you walk in!"

"Yeah, you all in here with the front door unlocked. Anybody could have come up in here! You must be Asher, right?" she smiled.

Asher stood up and walked over to Alisha. She reached her hand out to him. "I'm sure you've heard about me."

Asher looked at me with narrowed, questioning eyes, then back at Alisha.

"Oh, but I bet you heard about Corey, though, huh?" Alisha rolled her eyes.

"Oooh, the drama! I think I'm going to love it here." Asher smiled wide. "Actually, I met Corey yesterday."

Alisha sighed. "Yeah, she seems to be everywhere! But if she like it, I love it." She hunched her shoulders. "How are you liking Franklin so far?"

"No lies, it feels like home here," he admitted.

"Did Don tell you I'm the one who motivated her to lead this protest at the Capitol?" Alisha asked Asher, a proud smile on her face.

"No. But I know this one is near and dear to her heart because of her dad. No one has to tell me that."

Alisha's smile faltered. She glanced at me, confusion and something like hurt flashing across her face. "Her dad?"

I instinctively reached for my dad's dog tags and clutched them in my palms, feeling the raised letters press against my skin. I hadn't told her. For all our conversations about the protest and all the planning sessions, I'd never mentioned the real reason it mattered so much to me.

"Don, you okay?" Alisha touched me on my arm. Her voice was gentle, but I could hear the unspoken question: *Why didn't you tell me?*

I looked down at my hand wrapped around my necklace. Something about having both Asher and Alisha here, my past and my present colliding, made the words easier to find. Maybe it was time to stop compartmentalizing every part of my life.

"My dad, uh—" I exhaled and kissed the two military tags. "My dad was killed in Iraq."

My memory of him felt closer these days, as if he was watching over my shoulder as I worked on the protest plans. He'd always believed in standing up for people who couldn't stand up for themselves.

That's what my mom told me. She said it was the reason why he became a soldier in the first place—to help protect people. To help protect his country.

"Come on, girl." Asher wrapped his arms around me, and Alisha joined him.

"I am sorry, Don." She gave me the softest peck on my cheek.

I pulled away from their embrace and straightened my shirt.

"Thanks, y'all. I'm good. I just been in my feels since I started with all of this. I feel like my dad would be so proud of me for doing my part to try to save our soldiers who are over there in prison for no reason."

Asher shook his head, his eyes still warm and filled with concern as he stood next to me.

"Thank you for pushing me, Lish. It's just what I needed, honestly. I don't think I'd be doing any of this if it weren't for you."

Alisha's smile was bright. "You're not alone. I'm right here with you. We're going to see this through together." Our eyes held each other's gaze like magnets.

"Mmph! Well, okay." Asher broke the silence. "How much longer we gon' be in here?"

"No way!"

We all turned to see Devin standing at the door. He wasn't tall at all. At five six we stood eye to eye. But he had a personality that filled a room and made him seem seven feet tall, with a way of persuading us to see things his way without being demanding.

Devin was from Brazil and spoke Portuguese, Spanish, and English. His body was sculpted and chiseled, like a statue whose sculptor paid attention to the finest of details. His muscles were accentuated with the slightest of movements from him. They lined and curved with definition around his chest, arms, and legs.

Even in the chill and cold of autumn, he wore shorts. His skin was a flawless dark brown, which contrasted with his big light brown eyes that looked back at you with the curiosity of a baby.

He had the deepest dimples when he smiled, and curly jet-black hair that he kept low. It reminded me of the Jheri curl styles I'd seen on the R&B singers from my dad's old albums my mom kept, only his hair was naturally curly.

He probably could have been a professional model if he'd been taller. I found it easy to talk with him one-on-one because he had a strong, inviting energy about him.

"I see we are all locked in." He smiled, revealing a mouth full of shiny, silver braces. "I'm loving this! Why didn't you all text me and let me know you were still on campus?"

He sat next to Asher, who closed his eyes and took a deep breath. I held back my amusement.

"Hey, I'm Devin. People call me Dev. I haven't seen you around. Are you joining ACU or just our committee? We could certainly use the help."

"N-no, no, nah, I'm not—I'm not new. I—uh, I'm just, uh, I'm here visiting with Don."

Devin looked at me and then back at Asher.

"Okay, friend. Do you have a name?"

Asher chuckled at himself. "Right! Yes, I'm Asher. Nice to meet you, Dev." Their hands pressed together in a slow squeeze; their eyes focused on the other's.

"Same. Excuse my sweaty hands." He wiped his hands on his shorts. "I just came from a nice three-mile run; it's beautiful out today. No rain. You're here visiting, and you all are planning? Wow. What dedication. You must be down for the cause, then." He said it more like a statement than a question to Asher.

Asher sat up taller in his chair and clasped his hands in front of him on the table like he was in a formal interview. "No doubt." The words came out slow and unsure.

I almost failed to hold back my laughter.

"Good. Let me grab my things from the drawer. I know we have the Vice-Mayor committed, but I want the mayor and governor, too. Think that's too ambitious?" He looked at me and Alisha.

"Nothing beats a failure but a try!" Asher said.

I burst into laughter.

"You don't think it's impossible, huh?" Devin asked me. "I feel like being from Salvador, Bahia has taught me something. Governments everywhere try to silence those who challenge the system. That's why I chose this committee." His face was stern.

"No, I'm sorry; I don't think it's impossible at all. I think we should go all out. Make them tell us no."

"That's what I want to do, too," Alisha said. She turned to Devin. "I'm glad you're still here, Dev."

"Sem distrações," he replied after he talked about his friends heading to Chicago for break. He explained he wouldn't be flying back home to Brazil until winter break, preferring to stay focused on Operation Protect Those Who Protect Us. I was glad about that.

Our ideas collided and merged around the table like tributaries flowing into a river, separate streams of thought combining into something with enough force to move mountains—or at least city officials. After an hour of planning, we had our strategy.

Asher, unusually quiet except when Devin spoke, volunteered to take notes. We agreed to email and work to try set meetings with both the mayor and governor about the protest. It was a long shot, but we hoped they'd be present to speak or at least send out a message of support that said they stood with us.

"Now it's time to party!" Alisha declared, arms in the air.

"But where?" Asher chimed in; his eyes were wide, excited about the idea.

"Listen, I found this spot downtown. They don't check IDs as long as everyone stays chill, and they'll even serve us drinks. It's a hole in the wall, so you can't be acting like you go to Franklin when you see it," he warned. "Arrogante," he said, nose in the air, lips formed into a tight kiss. No translation needed; we all laughed in understanding.

"I love your language," Asher responded. "Can you teach me Portuguese?"

"Absolutamente." He shook his head. "Seja meu par hoje à noite."

"What does that mean?" Asher asked, as if staring at Devin's lips would somehow translate his words.

"Just say yes," Devin smirked, stacking papers into a neat pile in front of him.

"Yes." Asher responded without hesitation.

We agreed to meet in front of Nash-Jamison Hall an hour after we left Hester House.

"Dress casual. Nothing over the top. Remember, this is not a club," Devin instructed.

I texted Corey. She'd said she wanted to see me again. When I told her the plan, she asked who all was going to be there. My heart raced as I stared at her text. Having Corey and Alisha in the same space, especially after our kiss yesterday...I had reservations.

I typed Alisha's name and slowly deleted each letter, one by one.

I couldn't explain why, even to myself. I guess the thought of navigating whatever was happening between me and Corey while Alisha watched made my stomach twist. But I couldn't not invite Corey either, not after yesterday. I needed to see her again, to figure out if what I felt was real or just the heat of a moment.

I finally responded with everyone's name but Alisha's and shoved my phone into my pocket. It was break. We were just trying to have fun, I told myself. And despite this strange anxiety, I wanted them both to be there.

THE DOWN UNDER

Chapter Thirteen

Devin had us meet at Nash-Jamison Hall, insisting we walk rather than drive.

"It's not far," he'd assured us, "just about a mile off campus. Plus, nobody needs to worry about being the designated driver."

The spot seemed like a place only the locals would know about. It was behind a big Victorian-style home on a huge estate with plenty of land stretching for miles beyond the small hole-in-the-wall bar, which looked like a shack.

The path to it was paved with individual cobblestones that you had to tread carefully on, or your feet could land in wet mud, which was easy to do since there were no lights along its path. We illuminated our way with our cell phones.

"If I fuck up my J's, it's gon' be a problem," Alisha announced as we hopped from stone to stone.

"I told you to dress casual." Devin scoffed.

"This *is* my version of casual," she shot back.

"We're almost there," I intervened. "Just go slow."

Just behind us, Asher and Corey picked their way carefully along the path, oblivious to our bickering as they chatted about something that had Asher laughing every few steps.

From the outside, the tiny house didn't look like it could hold very many people, but it was surprisingly big inside. The backyard lights strung across the vaulted ceiling made the dim place feel even more illegal and hidden. All of the inside walls had been knocked down, so the place was wide open, filled with high top tables and bar stools.

People lined the walls and sat and stood at tables. Cigarette and cigar smoke made it almost impossible to breathe. The wooden bar stretched the entire length of the opposite wall with a sign that lit up above it: *The Down Under.*

I felt grown and independent, especially with Corey there. With her walking behind me, I was confident she was watching my ass with every step I took. I'd worn a pair of my tightest fitting, booty cuffing skinny jeans and a white tank top. My curly hair was down, and I was wearing just a pop of lip gloss.

I'd chosen my outfit carefully—something casual, but that made me feel good. The look was completed with my favorite ankle boots, giving me just enough height to feel confident but comfortable enough to dance in if the night went that way.

Corey had braided her Afro in cornrows again, which allowed me to see more of her face. She looked sexy as hell to me, even though she had on those beat up Chucks, a pair of blue jeans rolled up at the ankle, and an oversized plaid shirt that wasn't buttoned at the wrists.

The shirt sleeves flung open to reveal all those damn bracelets. But behind those glasses were the softest, sweetest eyes, accentuated by the blackest, curliest mascara-free eyelashes.

Asher and Devin headed immediately for the bar. I told Corey and Alisha I had to use the restroom.

"Me too," Alisha said, following behind me.

Corey shook her head and said, "I'll be at the bar," and headed after the guys.

"What the fuck, Don?" Alisha grilled me inside the bathroom that was really meant for one.

The space barely had room for one person, let alone two. With the door closed behind us, we were pressed together in the narrow space between the sink and wall, her face inches from mine.

She'd been giving me sideways glances ever since we left campus—and the way she had me pinned in, it was clear she couldn't wait to get me alone.

"What's wrong?" I asked. My face just inches from hers, our bodies pressed together so that neither one of us could turn or move without touching. Her back was pressed into the sink and mine into the wall where the window rested.

"What's wrong? I thought we had an understanding about not blowing me off for that girl."

I frowned. "How is this blowing you off?

"Don, your boy is all caked up with Devin. You're clearly on a date with ol' girl." She rolled her eyes. "And what am I?"

"My friend who I want to hang out with, too. Who didn't go home for break and should be here with me at this cool-ass spot we just learned about." I could feel her heavy breath on my face.

Her chest pressed against mine. I looked down at her breasts which pushed out over the edge of her V-shaped, sleeveless sweater. She watched my eyes linger there.

I began to perspire.

"Alright, Chandon. Fine." She turned around and began fixing her hair and checking her face in the mirror.

Her butt pressed against my crotch. I stood as still as I possibly could until she finished. She turned back toward me with a sideways smirk.

"Hurry up," she said.

I swallowed down the lump in my throat and suppressed the one that grew between my legs as she left me alone in the tiny bathroom.

I walked slowly from the bathroom to the bar. Devin and Asher were cozied up next to each other, laughing and talking. There was a highway of space between Alisha and Corey, and neither of them were speaking.

"What y'all decide to order?" I said, looking at the wall stacked full of liquor bottles, not knowing a thing about any of them. My heart started to race. It always did when I was out of my depth, the sudden awareness that I was faking my way through something everyone else seemed to understand instinctively.

"I got a Long Island iced tea," Alisha said, looking at me out of the corner of her eye.

"Oooh, that sounds like fun!"

"Girl, no. It's got like five different liquors in it. Yo' fresh off the tit ass can't handle that," Alisha laughed. She always acted like she'd been partying since middle school while I'd been home studying, which wasn't entirely wrong.

"Here, Freshy." Corey slid me a short glass filled with ice and what looked like red juice.

"What's this?" I took the glass with the skinny red straw into my hands and up to my lips.

"It's just vodka and cranberry. I didn't know what you like so I ordered that. Here." She scooted out the bar stool from in front of her and invited me to sit.

I looked over at Alisha, who was bobbing her head to the Reggaeton music playing. I sat and took a sip of my drink. Asher and I made eye contact, and he gave me a head nod and smile, darting his eyes between Alisha and Corey. He'd warned me not to invite Corey.

"You're just going to make it weird with Alisha there, too," he'd said. "Pick one or the other for tonight, don't try to juggle both." But I'd insisted I could handle it.

"There's nothing to juggle," I pushed back. "Alisha's just my friend."

"Okay, boo," was all he said, but his eyes told me what he wasn't saying: that he saw how I looked at Corey, that he remembered our excited dance around my dorm room after our kiss, and that he didn't want me messing up something good by trying to please everyone.

"So, how you like the drink?" Corey smiled at me, pulling me back to the present moment.

I looked at her lips and wanted to kiss them again.

"It's kind of strong," I admitted and took another sip.

She chuckled and took a sip of hers, too. Ours was the same.

"Hey." Corey placed her hand on my chin and turned my head. Her lips were pressed against mine and mine against hers. I felt my tongue slide into her open, waiting mouth. She sucked it in, and I closed my eyes, enjoying the music and her full lips.

"Y'all two love birds want another one?" We pulled apart and looked up at the woman bartender smiling at us.

She had a hoop earring on her eyebrow, one on her dark, purple-colored lips and wide nose, and several on both of her ears. Silver and gold rings adorned every finger. She had on a rainbow-colored tank top and denim overalls. Her jaw line was strong and perfect. She had a zigzag cut into the side of her fade.

"What y'all drinking? This one is on me." I recognized the gesture for what it was. A welcome to first-timers in a space that had probably been a sanctuary for her long before we found it.

Corey picked up her glass. "Um, cranberry juice and vodka. Thank you."

The bartender winked at her and began making the drinks.

"Is this a gay bar?" I asked, feeling really loose and free like I had no worries or cares.

Corey laughed at me, "You're so cute, Freshy. Yes! Look around." She looked around in dramatic fashion.

So did I, but intently. Ladies grinding on each other on the dance floor, men too. As a matter of fact, one of them was grinding on Alisha. My face flushed hot. I moved on quickly.

All types of people cuddled up or talking close. Young and old. Men together. Women together. People together. I suddenly felt emotional.

"Devin is so cool for this," I said barely above a whisper. "Did you know about this place?"

She shook her head no.

"Me either!" I said too loud. The bartender brought our drinks.

"You two be safe tonight, okay?" She smiled and moved on down the bar.

Asher plopped his shoulders right between Corey and me, one on her and one on me.

"Let's go dance! Come on!" He swayed his body to the music.

"Fuck it." I chugged my drink and stood up. I prodded Corey.

She chugged hers, and soon we were all on the dance floor where we bumped, grinded, swayed our hips, hugged close and tight, kissed, smiled and sang off beat to familiar songs, all huddled up in the too-small space reserved for dancing in the little shack house. We were in the middle of the dark, where we were free to be ourselves and let our souls collide.

We walked back in the pitch black of night, the mile-long trek to campus feeling much longer than it had on the way there, especially with the alcohol making my steps less certain. But we were all happier and louder than when we started. My hand grasped Corey's, swinging between us like schoolgirls.

Asher went back to the room with Devin. Alisha had some girl none of us had ever seen before wrapped around her shoulder, whispering in her ear and kissing her neck. Even though Corey held my hand tight, and I was excited to be with her, I watched them the entire time.

Back in my room, I grabbed both Corey and I bottles of water from the small fridge in my closet. I handed her one and gulped mine down immediately. I could feel her standing too close behind me. I was about to move to my bed when she gently grabbed my arm and pulled me back against my closet door. She stood in front of me, her eyes focused on mine.

"Freshy, why did you join ACU?" Her head was cocked to the side, her water bottle still unopened in her hand.

"Oh, no!" I tried to walk away. She put her arm up against the closet door to block me from moving. I turned, frozen, and looked back at her. Her eyes were still firmly fixed on mine, searching for something.

"Let's not ruin a—a perfectly good night with that shit." I grabbed her free hand and tried to pull her over to the bed. Her body was firm and poised. She did not move.

"See, I be noticing things. Is it because of that girl, Alisha? You were watching her the entire night. I saw you," she said, her voice low but intense. "I'm not stupid."

Something flickered in her eyes—a vulnerability beneath the challenge that made me pause. This wasn't just jealousy or possessiveness. This was fear.

"Corey, I feel like you just like arguing with me," I sighed.

I just wanted her lips on mine. Both of my lips. The ones talking and the ones between my thighs singing. They were both waiting.

"What I don't want to be is some young girl's fool or plaything. I'm not here for that."

"No! Stop it! I'm not a child," I said, my voice rising. "I know I'm Black. I don't need to join BSU for that, alright? Just because I have light skin doesn't mean I don't know who I am. I know who I am!"

"Who are you?" she asked with more curiosity than anger or frustration.

"I am exactly what you see," my voice was steady. "What do you see when you see me, Corey?"

"A beautiful Black woman," she said without hesitation.

"You either see me as Black and White or you don't see me at all, and that's the truth." I stared at her. "What? You too Black to be with me?"

"No. Chandon, I've been pulled into you from the moment I saw you."

She stepped close to me. The anger between us shifting into something electric. I wanted to wrap my arms around her and kiss her.

"No one's going to make me feel bad for being part of ACU. And no one's going to change my mind. I made a promise to my dad, and I'm going to keep it. You made a promise to your uncle, and I know you're going to keep yours, too. That's it. We don't owe anyone more than that."

"God, you're so fucking beautiful. You help me to see things I don't wanna see or I can't see. I grow every time I'm around you."

"You don't have to pick a fight with me to grow, Upper." I smiled.

"Upper?" She frowned. "What the hell is that supposed to mean?"

"Like upperclassman." I smiled wide at my own cleverness. "I'm Freshy and you're Upper."

I laughed, and she laughed. We fell into each other, laughing.

"You're too funny for that," she hollered in between gasps of laughter.

The heat of our touches smoldered between us. The laughter slowed. She pulled me in by my hips. Her slow grind on me was like electric currents between us. My arms wrapped tight around her neck, too afraid to let go. I moaned into her ear. She kissed my neck. My knees fell against hers. She held me up.

"I've been played before. I don't wanna be played by you," she whispered.

"I've been hurt before. I don't want to be hurt by you." I released my fear to her as well.

"I promise I won't hurt you, Freshy." She pulled me in closer. Her firm muscles tight around me. Her thighs interlocked with mine.

"I promise I won't play you, Upper."

Our lips met in a slow dance of promises. The taste of cranberry and vodka lingered between us, sweet and intoxicating. The distant bass from one of my dormmate's too-loud music vibrated through the walls, setting a rhythm our bodies instinctively found. We didn't move over to the bed, though. We stayed pressed against each other and the closet doors. Nothing else mattered.

I was an explosion of atmospheric pressure when she slid inside of me, her fingers going in smooth like she was meant to be there. We both allowed light moans to escape from the cracks of our waiting, longing lips. I was trapped in wonderment.

This feeling—this connection—was nothing like anything I'd experienced before. Not with Stephanie, not with anyone. Was this my fantasy realized or was I still dreaming about her? Had the alcohol heightened everything, or was this intensity just us, just what happened when all the arguing and tension finally broke?

At first, we stared at each other, saying nothing with our lips but everything with our eyes.

Then, she asked me—no, begged me—to let her keep going. I responded through moans of pleasure.

"Yes! Yes! Yes! God, please keep going."

But she waited. Right there inside me. Getting to know every part of me. My heartbeat dropped down from my chest and pulsed right around her fingers, pleading with her to join its rhythm. She fit into me like a glove.

"Oh my God," she whispered. Her eyes rolled shut.

She began kissing me soft and slow on my neck before she hoisted my thigh higher, gripping it more firmly in her strong hand. I could feel the muscles in her arm wrapped tight around my thigh. Her naked body pressed into mine, mine into the door. The cool wood against my back contrasted with the burning heat of her skin against my breast, belly, and thighs.

Every inch where we touched felt like a live wire, humming with electricity. The scent of her cocoa butter, mixed with something uniquely her, filled my lungs with each desperate breath. I was not going anywhere.

I wrapped my arms snug around her back and rested my head against the closet. I did all I could not to surrender and beg for her. Beg for her to go deeper. Lose me. Lose herself inside of me. I began to lose strength.

The waiting had me flowing like the Kintampo Waterfalls in East Ghana, a rushing, unstoppable force of nature I'd learned about in my African Studies class. Those falls—powerful enough to carve through stone over centuries yet creating something beautiful in their persistence—reminded me of this moment. Of us. Unstoppable. Transformative. Inevitable.

"You want it?" she asked, between runner's pants.

I didn't respond. My heart pounded against her chest. I knew she could feel it thumping. She slid in slower, further, deeper. Movements that teased me beyond ecstasy. The moans rushed out from me like escaped prisoners. I couldn't hold them in any longer. Her deep breathy murmurs followed mine.

"Tell me you want it." Her lips pressed against my ear. The hot air from her mouth moved down my body. I began to tremble. My thighs began to shake like mini earthquakes.

"I got you," she reassured me.

I swallowed hard and dug my fingers deep into her back. "Please," I begged.

She used her thigh to push her hand deeper inside of me. I released sounds of pleasure without regard. I was so loud. I didn't care. She stopped abruptly.

In that moment, I was snatched from my journey to outer space, where I'd be able to lay in a bed of stars.

I jerked my body like a baby throwing a tantrum. *Give it to me!* She chuckled at my collapse into her. But she was strong enough to hold me up. We faced each other again. I could feel the nectar from her inner thighs run down my leg. This wasn't one-sided, she wanted me as desperately as I wanted her. It stripped away my last defense, the last wall I'd built to protect myself.

"I want... to hear...you say...you want...me," she whispered.

We stared at each other. I was afraid to let it all go. My body had already betrayed me, collapsing into weak trembles. I looked deeper into her eyes, where my fears were calmed and melted away. Melted away into her grip. Melted away into her touch.

I exhaled.

"I want you," I pleaded. "I want you." I sang it over and over until our bodies bounced and gyrated and danced into their maximum rhythm of ecstasy.

I floated past the moon with her right there next to me, our bodies becoming constellations of sensation, mapping new territories of pleasure neither of us had charted before. We held each other's hands among the stars, tethered to each other as we soared through this discovered universe.

As we began our descent back to earth, our chests heaved against each other's. Both of us calmed our breathing again. The warm air rushed from our opened mouths. Our fingers locked and intertwined together.

My legs were too weak to hold me up any longer. We slid to the floor. She announced feeling the chill against her back. My ear pressed into her chest. It listened as her heart slowed. She wrapped her arms around me. I felt safe.

Never let me go. I wanted to say those words as they came to me. So, I did.

"Never let me go," I crooned.

"I promise." She kissed my forehead to seal the deal.

Chapter Fourteen

For the rest of the week, I hardly got to hang out with Asher alone; he was either with Devin somewhere or in Devin's room. I had no time to complain because I was curled up under Corey like a baby. Every chance we got, our bodies joined together, and we took a trip to the stars.

When we weren't in outer space, we were at Hester House focused and planning the protest.

Corey had surprised me by showing up to help us.

"I know this matters to you," she'd said simply, sliding into the chair beside me. "And if it matters to you, it matters to me."

Though she'd never been particularly invested in ACU's causes before, she threw herself into the work with the same intensity she brought to everything else. It wasn't just about supporting me, I could see her genuinely connecting with the injustice of two Black women veterans being imprisoned for who they loved.

Alisha's friend was there, too. The girl she met at The Down Under. She lived in town and wasn't a student at Franklin or the junior college up the road. In fact, she didn't even know if she was ever going to college. She worked at a drugstore and had a roommate.

She was mostly on her phone when Alisha brought her to Hester House and rarely helped with anything. *Whatever*, I thought. But Tammy was cool enough. Corey tried to engage her in conversation or pull her into the work, but she didn't seem like the type to be persuaded to do anything she didn't want to do. One day, I stood near them as they spoke.

"I'm cool off this college stuff. If I wanted to go to college, I would have. Different strokes for different folks," she told Corey plainly while chewing her gum and moving her eyes between her phone and the conversation.

"But what about in a few years, when you're in your mid-twenties?"

"I like to live in the moment. Right now, I'm not even a year out of high school. I need a break. You seem like you could use one, too."

We all chuckled as we sat at the round table strategizing and eavesdropping on their conversation.

"Where I'm from in Brazil," Devin added, leaning forward, "people protest differently. More dancing, more music, but the stakes are just as high. Sometimes higher." He glanced at me.

"That's why I respect what you're doing here. You're using the tools this country gives you to change it. That's something I came here to learn more about. Age doesn't matter when it comes to facing and changing injustice." He looked at Tammy.

Tammy shrugged, not looking up. "To each their own I guess."

What did Alisha see in her? I caught myself judging Tammy's appearance, thinking she'd be prettier without the weave covering her small-framed face, the gel slicked along her eyebrows and cheeks, the bright makeup, the drawn-on eyebrows, the Betty Boop lashes, and pink lipstick. I tried to picture her "natural" and decided her chestnut-colored skin and slanted eyes didn't need all that.

Then I realized how I sounded, even in my own head, like a privileged person who thought they knew better than everyone else about how to look "appropriate." Who was I to decide what looked good on her?

But even as I reminded myself what Alisha once told me—*if you like it, I love it*—I couldn't help wondering if Alisha even liked it, let alone *loved* it.

"Let's do a double date," Alisha said to me.

"You for real?" I stopped writing on the posterboard and put the marker on the table.

"Yep." She popped her lips. "I think it'll be cute!" She smiled wide. Her eyes twinkled back at me.

"Hey, Asher," I yelled across the table. "Alisha wants us all to go out on a double date."

"That would make it less double and more triple," she said, staring at me.

I smiled. "Even better."

"I'm down," Devin replied, smiling at Asher, who smiled back at him. They acted like they had been together for more than the few days Asher had been on campus.

"Well, my funds are drying up. Pops has not made any deposits into my account since this impromptu detour," Asher confessed.

"I got you, meu bebê." Devin winked, and Asher swooned.

"Where to?" Corey swiveled around in her chair and chimed in.

"Oooh, Applebee's!" Tammy finally looked up from her phone.

"Applebee's it is," Alisha said.

At Applebee's we sat at a long booth by the window. The restaurant buzzed with the Friday night crowd, the air thick with the smell of fryer oil and sweet cocktails. Pop music competed with the clatter of dishes and loud conversation.

Alisha and I sat in front of each other, closest to the window. Corey sat next to me and Asher sat next to her. Tammy looked squeezed in tight between Alisha and Devin.

Asher and Devin held hands across the table while Corey's hand crept up my thigh.

"I got something for us." Tammy pulled a flask from her purse, unscrewed the silver cap, and took a swig. Her face contorted and she hissed as the liquor went down.

I frowned. "What's that?"

"Tequila," Tammy said it as if it were obvious.

"Yeah, tequila, *Freshy!*" Alisha grabbed the flask and took a sip like she was a pro.

Corey glared at her. I felt her hand squeeze my thigh, which made me jump.

"Y'all getting freaky at the table," Asher blurted out, nudging Corey with her elbow.

"Not a bad idea." Corey kissed my cheek.

Alisha shoved the flask into my hand.

"Your turn, *Freshy*," she smirked.

Corey sat up, "Would you—"

I took a big gulp and acted like the liquor didn't burn a hole into my esophagus as it flowed into my belly. I passed it to Corey.

"Here, your turn!" I said all too quick.

"Nah, I'm good." She passed the bottle to Asher.

"What? You got tutoring after this?" Alisha teased.

Tammy and Alisha giggled. Corey snatched the bottle from Asher.

"Matter of fact, the only thing I got to do is you, Freshy." Corey took a sip, then leaned over and sucked on my neck, which would have felt good under different circumstances. She took another sip and passed it on.

"Let's go to the bar and get a drink." Devin passed the flask back to Tammy without drinking from it.

"We can't get a drink from the bar. We're not twenty-one," Asher said.

"No, *you're* not twenty-one. I am!" Devin flashed an ID.

Asher snatched it and inspected it. "Is this real?" he asked.

"Nope!" Devin snatched it back.

"Hell yeah, let's go."

The four of us sat at the table, quiet.

"Awkward," Tammy sang, before she pulled out her phone and started scrolling.

"So, y'all a couple now?" Alisha asked, her eyes darting between me and Corey.

I looked at Corey. Corey cleared her throat.

"Aren't you two friends? Why not ask her directly?"

"This is me asking her directly. Y'all seem glued at the hip now. I can't get a minute of her time anymore, so I'm asking now."

Something flashed in her eyes when she looked at me—not just concern, but something else I couldn't quite name. She quickly masked it with that forced smile.

"You're so jealous," Corey said, low but loud enough for Alisha to hear her.

I squirmed in my seat.

"Of my friend? No. But I definitely got her back." Alisha leaned her face in toward Corey for emphasis.

Corey released an exasperated sigh. "I'm going to the bar with the fellas."

I waited until Corey was out of ear shot.

"Are you okay?" I asked, leaning toward Alisha.

"Y'all must've hooked up before," Tammy said. She picked up the menu. "This is crazy. Look, I'm going to eat with y'all, but then I'm out."

"No, why?" Alisha pressed her body into Tammy's and leaned her head on her shoulder.

"The vibes is off."

I smirked and turned away. *It's so obvious she does not like that girl,* I thought to myself.

"Lish, what's going on?" I pleaded.

"Look, I tried to give the girl a chance; I just don't like her. I think she's fake. How she go from embarrassing you to fucking you? That's crazy."

"Why do you care," Tammy chirped.

"'Cause she my friend and I don't want her to get hurt."

"I'm not going to get hurt," I shot back.

"Look, just don't call me when you sitting in your room all scared to walk around campus again."

"That won't happen." I looked down at my menu.

"Sure, girl."

Chapter Fifteen

Change was in the air. November edged out October, carrying off the last stubborn leaves. The campus burned in fiery oranges and reds, a quiet reminder that nothing stays the same for long.

"Either way," Asher said, stuffing clothes into his duffle bag, "You're gonna have to choose. Alisha and Corey in the same room is like mixing bleach and ammonia." He stopped packing momentarily. "Somebody's gonna die," he laughed at himself as he continued to pack.

I sighed. I couldn't laugh. The truth of it was all too real for me.

It was Sunday morning. He was packing up the last of his belongings, heading back to New Jersey. He'd already submitted his transfer application to Franklin for the upcoming fall semester.

"I'm finishing out this year because my dad would actually kill me if I just quit mid-year," he'd explained. "But I'm coming here next fall, even if I have to take out loans."

I sat on my bed and watched him stuff his unfolded things into his duffle bag on the floor. My heart was heavy with sadness. The more items he stuffed into it, the sadder I became. When he packed the Franklin University sweatshirt Devin had given him—already a prized possession after just a week—the reality that he was leaving hit me.

"Alisha has had my back, Ash."

"Now Corey's got it." He gave me a sly look, clapped his hands together, and hollered. "Seriously, just work together and finish up the protest to the Capitol. Y'all will be ok."

"You believe that?"

"No, but I will if you really need me to!" He laughed again.

"You're such an asshole." I stood and gave him a playful muff to his head.

"So, you'll be back in February for the protest then?"

He smacked his lips, "You know it! I'm going to have to get a part-time job because I'm all in on Operation—what's it called?" He snapped his fingers in an attempt to recall the name.

"It's called Operation Get Back to Devin!" I slapped his arm with laughter.

"Whatever." He waved me off. "Shit, with all that work I put in on *my* break? Chile, yes! I'm definitely coming back!"

"Yeah, you were putting in work alright!" I laughed.

He stood from his packing. "I just might be in love, Don." He pressed his hands into his chest. "Dev is the sweetest guy I've ever dated."

"For a *week*," I reminded him.

"Love has no time limits, just like it doesn't always start off smooth." With pursed lips, he blinked his eyes at me what seemed like one thousand times.

"Touché."

I picked up his book bag; he swung his duffle back over his shoulder.

He turned back toward me. "Don, seriously. Corey—I like her." He shrugged. "She's fine as hell! And I won't forgive you for not telling me that part! Anyway, listen, she might've started off rocky, but just the way she looks at you, whew chile!" He fanned himself. "Busted up shoes or not, she is gorgeous and smitten with you."

I opened my mouth to speak. He put his finger up to hush me.

"And I'm happy to see you like her, too. So don't fuck it up!" He laughed. "I'm just kidding." He paused. "No, I'm not." He laughed at himself again and walked toward the door, paused at the mirror, and checked his attire.

"Asshole," I whispered.

"I heard that," He sang.

"I know," I sang back.

Even though Asher hadn't worked directly on our protest plans, losing him felt like losing a crucial ally at the worst possible time. Fall break was over, and already the semester was speeding toward the finish line.

Our planned march to the Capitol would happen just after we got back from winter break, if we could pull everything together in time. And somehow, without Asher around, everything ahead felt heavier, like I'd have to figure it out on my own.

I could almost hear my dad's voice. Or maybe just the version of it I'd built in my head, saying, *"I got you, baby girl."* That's what my grandmother always said he used to whisper when he carried me around the house. I reached for my dog tags and held them close, letting myself believe I wasn't as alone as I felt.

Chapter Sixteen

Finals loomed, winter break crept closer, and February rushed at us like a deadline we couldn't outrun.

Nestled in the crook of Corey's arm, wrapped tight in my dorm bed, I let the midafternoon sunlight remind me of how much was still waiting — Dr. Collier's class, protest meetings, endless checklists. But with Corey, time always seemed to stand still.

The protest planning had kicked into high gear. We were six weeks out from the march to the Capitol, and every part of my life revolved around it. Designing posters, coordinating with local businesses, reaching out to media outlets. It was exhausting. It was consuming. But with Corey by my side, it felt like it mattered even more.

She'd surprised everyone by becoming one of our strongest organizers, using her BSU connections to open doors we couldn't have reached on our own. Just last week, she got us a meeting with the mayor's chief of staff.

"See? I told you we're stronger together," she whispered after the meeting, squeezing my hand.

In moments like that, it was hard to separate what I felt for her from the movement we were building. They had grown tangled together, each feeding the other.

Whenever we could steal a moment between classes, meetings, and late-night strategy sessions, we did. We hadn't made anything official after finally giving in to everything between us, and after the hottest night of my life, but it sure felt official to me.

Winter break was coming fast, and now February was bearing down hard. Every day felt heavier than the last, like it carried the weight of the whole movement on its back.

Every night we spent together, every strategy session where our minds synced, every moment she defended me against skeptics who still remembered our yard confrontation, it all felt like we were building something real. Something lasting. That's why her next words hit me like a slap.

"I—I think this thing between us might be coming to an end for a while."

She peeled our bodies apart and sat up. Jolted, I sat up too.

"What do you mean?"

She was silent. She moved her legs from under the covers and placed them on the floor, her bare muscular back toward me.

"What time did you say your roomie might come back?" She dodged the question.

"I don't know." I hunched my shoulders. "Answer my question, please." I ran my fingers through my tousled curls, tangled from how she liked to hold on to them.

She turned back toward me, one leg still out of the bed, the other folded on it. She held my hands.

"Freshy—I mean, Chandon." My heart skipped a beat as she stumbled over my name.

She looked down at our joined hands before meeting my eyes again.

"Listen, I'm going to California next semester," she said, her voice steadier now.

"The National Black Justice Coalition at Berkeley accepted me into their program. I'll be researching policy on police violence, racial profiling—" her voice caught in her throat. "Everything that happened to my uncle."

My chest felt hollow, emptied by her words. California. Next semester. Each syllable hammered against my ribs like a physical blow. I pulled her close, pressing my ear to her chest, where her heartbeat steadily, reliably, unlike mine, which seemed to have forgotten its rhythm entirely.

All our plans for the protest crumbled in my mind, her standing beside me at the podium, her voice joining mine as we demanded justice. The speech we'd planned to write together. The victory we'd imagined sharing. I'd be doing it alone.

But beneath the shock and hurt, something else stirred, a realization that cut deeper than her leaving. This was who Corey was. She would always chase the bigger fight, the next cause, the wider impact. Loving her meant loving that fire in her, even when it carried her away from me.

My grandfather had wanted me to find my people, my purpose. I'd found both in Corey, but I hadn't expected how much it would hurt when those things pulled us in different directions.

I sat motionless, my hands slipping from hers. The room tilted around me.

"It's only for a select few students from across the nation," she continued in the silence. "I already accepted it—before us, before this. It's bigger than me, Chandon."

I hopped out of bed and began putting my clothes on.

"Yeah, before me and you. And what are we, again? A *thing*? A *this*?"

"What? No!"

"That's what you just said." I picked my sweater up from the floor and swung it over my head and through my arms. I stopped moving. "I mean, I'm happy for you. Of course, I am. It sounds amazing. And—and you get to work on policy related towards changing police laws and practices. This is great." I tried not to choke on the words.

I continued getting dressed. She reached for my arms and pulled me in close.

"Freshy, look at me. It's only for a semester." She searched my eyes.

"You should probably get dressed, too. She'll be coming in soon for her afternoon nap." My roommate was like clockwork with her schedule. I loved and hated her for it.

Corey hurried into her clothes. She jumped into her shirt and pants, then pulled me over to the messy bed. Our knees touched. My hands were in hers again.

"Listen, I'll be back. I mean, I'm there over the summer, too, but I'll be back in the fall for the new school year."

"This is crazy," I ran my hands through my hair. My fingers got all caught up in the tangles, just like my thoughts were getting caught on this bombshell she'd just dropped. "I just need a moment to process this, that's all."

"Of course you do, of course you do. But you can visit me in the summer."

"In California? How?" I looked at her like she'd lost her damn mind. California might as well have been another planet.

"Get a job, Freshy! Save your money, get a ticket and come see me this summer. I'll take you to the beach." She smiled with those perfect teeth, her eyes all lit up with possibilities I couldn't see. All I could picture was the map from Tennessee or Illinois to California, stretching out way too far, with way too many states between us.

She wrapped her arms around me, but I pushed her away. I didn't want her touch right now.

Her promises about texting and calling sounded hollow, like when people said "let's keep in touch" but knew it was bullshit.

Something shifted inside me then. Not breaking, exactly, but cracking open. The tears I'd been fighting finally won, spilling down my cheeks before I could stop them.

"You're scared we won't make it." I said it like a statement.

Her chin rested on top of my head as I surrendered to her embrace, her heart beating against mine. I could feel myself standing at the edge of something scary as hell, loving someone who was about to be out of reach.

"I love you, Corey."

She kissed my forehead, her lips warm against my skin.

"I know you love me, Freshy. But sometimes love ain't enough to stop things from going wrong."

We swayed together like we were slow dancing but with no music. Just promises being exchanged.

"Do you love me?" I looked into her eyes, needing something real to hold onto.

"You don't know that by now?"

"Say it." I waited.

"I love you."

I guided her hand into my unzipped pants.

"Take me to the stars," I whispered, looking into her eyes. My fingers curling around hers, anchoring us before the gravity of reality pulled her away.

"What about your roommate?"

"I don't care," I moaned.

Chapter Seventeen

Winter break had officially begun. We stood outside, waiting on Corey's taxi, the cold air pressing against us like an unwelcome guest. The dorms were half-empty, the campus quiet, the weight of break settling in. Most students had already left, their goodbyes exchanged days ago. But me and Corey? We lingered.

We stayed on campus until the last possible second, stretching time like a rubber band about to snap. Still, it wasn't enough. She was heading home to D.C., then off to California, and I hadn't even had a chance to wrap my mind around it. Everything just kept moving forward, but it felt like my heart had hit pause.

Asher texted to say he was already home, which gave me something to look forward to. A month of hanging with him.

But Corey? What would we have? Just texts, calls, and Face-Time. No touching. No kissing. No waking up tangled together.

Just waiting. Until summer. If I could scrounge up the money for a flight. She agreed to help, but summer felt like a lifetime away.

From Willowbrook, Illinois, to Washington, D.C., I knew every way to get there. Eleven hours by car, a whole day by train, three by bike, 253 hours on foot, or two hours on a direct flight. Pointless knowledge, but I held onto it like it meant something.

"I don't wanna leave you, Freshy."

"Then don't." My voice cracked, barely above a whisper.

Bare trees lined the sidewalk, their branches clawing at the gray sky. Our breath fogged in the cold air, curling between us like smoke. I pressed my forehead to hers, trying to hold her here just a little longer. Corey's lips brushed against mine, soft, slow, like she was memorizing the way we fit together.

"I'll be back soon. It's just a plane ride away." She said it like I could just hop on a flight and be there in an instant.

I shut my eyes to her words.

"Hey, hey, look at me, Freshy." Her hands, cold against my face, as she lifted my chin. "We'll figure it out."

Her taxi pulled up. Time was officially up. I pouted on purpose, pushing my bottom lip out.

"No sulking," she scolded, smiling like she wasn't breaking my heart.

"I can if I want to." A weak laugh slipped out, but it didn't make me feel any better.

She kept talking about how I'd have more time to focus on ACU, the protest, school. Like that was supposed to make it easier. I nodded like it did.

"By the time you're back, you'll be counting down to the Capitol. You've got Leslie's number, right?"

I shook my head. Of course, she'd thought of that. Leslie was stepping in as BSU's interim president while Corey was gone, but nobody could fill the space she left behind. The driver slammed the trunk shut, then tapped it twice. The signal. I grabbed her hand and held it tight. Like I could hold onto her and stop her from leaving.

"If you stayed, you'd see it all. Please, I don't think I can do this without you."

She smirked, tracing slow circles on my palm. "You already are, Freshy. And that? That's sexy as hell." She smiled that charming ass smile of hers.

Our lips met again, urgent this time. The taxi honked, yanking us back to reality.

"We have to make noise," she murmured against my mouth. "We can't let them kill us, jail us, and stay silent about it."

"I know," I mumbled, but she finished the quote anyway.

"If you are silent about your pain, they'll kill you and say you enjoyed it." The famous words of Zora Neale Hurston, quoted by Dr. Collier. Words Corey lived by. Words I had no choice but to live by, too.

"If I were here, I'd be right next to you. You know that."

"Exactly, Corey. But you won't be."

Her fingers brushed against the dog tags under my layers. Her trump card. "If that were you or I locked up over there just for loving each other, what would we want people to do for us?"

I sighed. She had me. "I love you." The only thing I knew for sure.

"I love you, too." She kissed me one last time, lingering like she wanted to make it last.

"And I know you'll be loud. You'll make national news."

One more kiss. One last second. Then she was in the car. Then she was gone. I stood there, frozen, watching until the taxi turned the corner. I thought about my dad, about the silent promise I made a long time ago, even if I didn't have the words for it back then. It was clearer to me now.

To be someone he'd be proud of. To keep going, even when the weight of goodbye tried to break me.

Corey was gone. But Monica Jacobs and Lorraine Cuttleston were still out there, locked in prison cells in a foreign country. Still waiting. And I still had work to do.

The tears came fast, burning my cheeks, but I let them fall. Let them say what I couldn't.

Falling for her had been so complicated and easy all at the same time, like trying to hold onto a basketball mid-dribble. Right there in your hands one second, spinning away the next.

Now that we were together, losing her, even for a few months, felt impossible.

The wind picked up, cutting sharply against my face.

My phone buzzed in my pocket. I wiped my eyes with the sleeve of my coat. Before I could check it, I heard a voice behind me, one I hadn't really talked to in weeks.

"When does your flight leave, Don?"

I turned around.

Alisha stood beside two massive suitcases, bundled up in a red bubble coat, her black hat's tassels swaying. Ready for the Midwest winter.

Things had been distant between us since Corey. Just check-ins and conversations about the protest, nothing personal.

But now here she was in the cold, with me.

I didn't say anything at first. Just let the sight of her settle into the space Corey had just left.

It wasn't everything.

But maybe it was a start.

Chapter Eighteen

It was freezing cold back home, just as I expected. The kind of cold that crept through coats slid under scarves, and bit at your bones. But that didn't stop me and Asher from running around like we had the city to ourselves. Movies, the mall, kicking it at each other's houses, we did it all.

For the first time, we rode the "L" with no adults, the steel-on-steel screech of the train made it feel like we were stepping into real independence. That feeling we'd gotten used to at Franklin… that feeling followed us home.

One day, we wandered around downtown, staring up at the skyscrapers like we hadn't been seeing them all our lives. We even scrounged up enough to eat at Harry Caray's inside Water Tower. Grown.

I ended up texting Lish. I missed our friendship, and being away from Franklin felt like the perfect time to fix that. We met up at Harold Washington Library to work on protest plans, then spent the rest of the day at Navy Pier, drinking hot cocoa as the wind tried to snatch the cups from our hands.

We rode the Ferris wheel, the city sprawling beneath us, lights flickering against the water. It was so cold I swore the metal would freeze, trapping us up there with the sky and the birds.

"See, this is *my* city," she said with pride. "This why you can't claim Chicago if you not *from* Chicago." Lish smirked, stretching her arms across the tiny box we sat in.

I ignored the jab, eyes roaming over the skyline. The wheel inched along, slow like a stretched-out heartbeat. It scared me, thrilled me, and made me grateful to be in the moment. I took a million pictures, including a few of me and Lish making faces, wrapped in hats and scarves. I sent some to Corey. She didn't respond.

Being home grounded me in a way I didn't realize I needed. Sleeping in my bed. Laughing with Asher. Walking streets where everything felt familiar. But even with the comfort, there was tension. My grandfather had heard about the protest through his Franklin connections. Some of his friends he graduated with sat on the board, taught classes, or had relatives in attendance, too.

"I think it's a noble cause, Donny." That was all he said. But there was a lot buried in that curt response.

We sat in his dining room, and the whole family gathered at the long wooden table. My grandmother beamed at me across the table.

"I knew you'd do well, Donny, but this? This is fantastic." Then her tone shifted, teasing. "Is there some young gentleman who's inspired you?"

I stared down at my plate, biting back the truth. I wondered if it was a good time to tell my grandparents, especially my grandfather, that I was inspired by a gentle*woman* instead. The words built up inside me, pressing against my ribs, my pulse picking up. Just as the courage solidified, ready to spill out, Aunt Ronda chimed in.

"Girl, I sho' nuff wasn't doing nothing like this as a freshman," Aunt Ronda cut in, laughing. "Cover your ears, Mama and Daddy." She leaned in towards me, "I was too busy smoking weed, partying, and running from Daddy's rules."

"Wasting our money," my grandfather grumbled.

"Hey, I graduated! I got the most out of your money if you ask me." She grinned, eyebrows bouncing at him playfully.

"Not me." Uncle Dee puffed his chest, sitting up taller. "I was on the debate team, golf team, pledged the same as Daddy, and still made Dean's List."

Ronda rolled her eyes and let out a loud yawn.

That was what I hadn't missed. The competition. Trying to measure up to my grandfather's impossible standards. He was a veteran. A civil rights activist. He'd built one of the biggest law firms in Illinois. How could anyone ever be enough for him?

And not once while I was home did lumberjack Carl—my mom's maybe-boyfriend—stop by. The one E.J had warned me about. I wanted to ask her, but every time we were alone, my mind went straight to Dad, and I couldn't do it. Couldn't bring myself to hear her talk about moving on.

By the time break ended, I was ready to get back to Franklin. I missed my independence. I even missed my dorm room. The city approved our permit during the break—Operation Protect Those was happening. Independent news outlets were talking about Monica Jacobs and Lorraine Cuttleston, but no one on national TV. Yet. That would change.

Corey had been in California for almost a couple of weeks. She sent pictures: her new campus, the Golden Gate Bridge, the ocean, in front of Zellerbach Hall where her cohort was invited to see Alvin Ailey American Dance Theater perform.

I wish you were here. She texted.

Me too. I sent a sad-face emoji.

That was Thursday. I texted her again Friday morning. No response. I called Friday night and left a voicemail. I told myself she was just busy with her internship. But something gnawed at me. I needed to talk to her about what we would walk into when we got back to school.

Threats. Emails. Social media comments. Even letters were sent straight to the school and Hester House. Anti-gay groups, extreme religious conservatives. Furious that we were fighting for two women they claimed had broken the law. That we were wasting resources on criminals. That we should be focusing on school instead of "wasting taxpayers' dollars".

We called an emergency ACU meeting in the Marsha P. Johnson room.

"We should make this known school wide." Chris, our president, leaned against the wall, arms crossed. "We have majority support. If we get folks riled up, administration will have to say something. They're too damn quiet."

"We can't take this shit lightly," Lisa added. "They're dangerous."

"We should just keep focused," Antonio, our secretary, countered. Antonio's broad shoulders seemed to carry the weight of the room, his dark complexion glowing under the soft lights of Hester House, deep laugh lines framing his eyes despite his serious expression. "Two thousand followers mean we're already gaining traction."

"Hell no." Alisha slammed her palm on the table. "These MAGA motherfuckers aren't playing. This is our lives."

Chris shifted, exhaling through his nose and rolling his eyes before turning away. "These aren't new tactics. They're trying to scare us. We can't let them."

"But telling people could bring more threats," Shelly, our VP, added softly. Shelly's delicate fingers tapped nervously on the table, her wire-framed glasses sliding down her nose every few minutes. "This is supposed to be peaceful."

All eyes landed on me. My heart pounded as I realized they were waiting for me to break the tie—the freshman they'd once dismissed held the deciding vote. I took a breath.

"Our classmates deserve to know what we're facing," I said, finding my voice growing stronger with each word. "But we need a strategy. Chris and Shelly, talk to admin first. Let's see if we have their support. Then we decide how to tell everyone else."

I thought of Corey. The elevator. Her words. We ring the alarm, so people know there's a problem. Standing still? Being quiet? That was the real danger.

"What we are not going to do is stop." My voice came out sharper than expected.

Murmurs of agreement. Nods. Hands stacked in the center of the table.

"On three: Protect Those Who Protect Us."

Determination settled in. But as I left, I checked my phone. No response from Corey.

I texted again. *Hope you're settling in. Crazy stuff happening here. Call me.*

Nothing.

"You scared?" Lish had snuck up on me as I walked back to my room, my phone still in my hand.

I sighed. "A little. Actually, a lot. This shit is crazy."

"Where I'm from, you take threats seriously."

I nodded. "But it's always been college students."

"What?"

"Young people fought in the Civil Rights and Black Power movements. Dr. King…Malcolm X…they never saw forty."

She studied me, then grinned. "You be knowing your shit, girl."

She slowed her stride. "You okay? You seemed distant after our meeting."

I shrugged. "Just tired."

"Is that all?"

I hesitated. "Yeah. And classes. This semester is kicking my ass."

She nudged me. "Want a study buddy?"

I smiled. "That would be nice."

Chapter Nineteen

The time had flown by. We were two days away from the protest, and Corey still hadn't called. I kept telling myself she was busy, but the silence was loud. So, when I opened my door and saw Asher standing there, I broke. I swung the door to my room open and jumped into his waiting arms.

"Oh, my God! You actually came!" My voice cracked as the warmth of his hug wrapped around me. Tears pricked my eyes. Between the protest planning and my strained silence with Corey, my emotions had been a mess.

"Boo, I told you I was coming." We pulled apart, and he smirked.

"Yeah, but how?" My eyes scanned him like the answer might be written somewhere on his hoodie.

"Still got my pop's emergency credit card, that's how. But probably not for long." He tossed his duffle bag onto the floor, stepping into my room. "Maybe he'll find out and blow a damn fuse. Probably start talking about how I should be focusing on school, finding the right girl, 'building my future,' all that bullshit. But whatever. I'm here."

He paused when he noticed my roommate at her desk. "Oh."

I folded my legs onto my bed. "Ash, this is Tiffany. Tiffany, this is my best friend in the whole world, Asher the Great!" I beamed.

She turned, pulling her headphones from her ear. "Hi, Asher. Nice to meet you. Chandon tells me you're at an Ivy League but transferring here?"

"Yeah, I am." Asher nodded. "I'll be a Franklinite next year!"

Tiffany arched a brow. "Huh. That's interesting. Most people start here and go on to the Ivies for grad school. You know, set a strong foundation to deal with all that's ahead, including being twice as good. That's my plan, anyway."

Asher looked at me, then back at her.

"If I had the choice, I would've done the same, but—"

"But you're already in, so you might as well tough it out. Why are you transferring, anyway?"

His lips tightened, then he shrugged. "My own personal journey, I guess."

Tiffany nodded slowly, her tone shifting. "Like this protest? I don't even understand how you," she turned toward me, "or you, to be honest, have time for this."

Asher slid his bag over by my bed. "This? Two Black women—veterans—who served this country, so we can choose this school or that one. And they're being held on some bullshit just because they're gay."

Tiffany turned fully toward us.

"They knew the laws before they went there, didn't they? Why would two U.S. veterans go to a country that criminalizes their very identity? And now students are wasting time fighting to bring them home? Ridiculous."

I stood up. "Tiffany, you have no idea what you're talking about. You can't be so focused on school that you ignore everything going on around you. Isn't the point of college to grow socially, too? You're a hermit stuck in your little world, trying to become a doctor and change your social class. Open your eyes!"

"You've said a lot of nothing," she replied blankly.

"Oh, my God," Asher groaned, rubbing his forehead.

"Well, maybe they wouldn't have had to go to a country like Kuwait if, after serving and sacrificing their lives, this country didn't still discriminate against them."

I clapped my hands with emphasis at the end of the last three words: "Discriminate. Against. Them."

"Facts," Asher added.

"Black veterans have higher rates of unemployment, lack of access to mental health services, trouble finding jobs, and are underrepresented in leadership roles within the military. Maybe that's why two Black women, who already served, would leave their country for a place like Kuwait."

"Facts." Asher's voice punctuated my point.

I exhaled, relieved to get some of my research off my chest. I had learned so much while preparing for my speech at the Capitol. It helped me understand why my father took that contracting job at the start of the war and why he kept choosing service. This protest wasn't just about those two women, it was about every Black veteran ignored after they'd given everything.

Tiffany turned back around, stuffing her books into her backpack.

"That's why I study the way I do. I'm trying to start my own private practice, so I don't have to work for anyone but Tiffany Yvette Donaldson." She checked her watch. "I have a study session. Good luck."

Asher stepped aside, letting her pass. Then, once the door clicked shut—

"Oh, my God, Don!"

I shook my head. "I know. I'm so tired of justifying what we're doing—to random people, to Franklinites, to folks in the community when we're handing out flyers. Like, fuck! What happened to all that patriotism? Is it only for straight people?"

"Straight, White people. Other parts sold separately," he deadpanned.

I chuckled as he plopped onto my bed next to me, kicking his shoes off.

"The flights were long as hell. I picked the cheapest route to save money and maybe avoid Pops yelling at me too much, which meant three damn layovers. I need a shower and a nap." He yawned. "I thought you said your roommate was cool?"

"No, I said it's cool that she's never really here." I laughed. "We don't even talk like that. Guess she felt like sharing today."

"Sooo, how are things with you and Devin?"

His grin stretched wide. "We're thinking of getting an apartment off-campus next year."

My jaw dropped. "What the—"

"I know, I know. Crazy, right? But I like him so much, Don! We talk all night and text all day! We're hanging out tonight, which is why I need this shower and nap."

"Does he even know you're here?"

"Girl, no! He'd want to see me immediately, and I am not ready for that." He gestured to his outfit—black joggers, a sweatshirt, and a jacket. Perfectly fine, in my opinion.

He peeled off his jacket and slid under my blankets. "I'm so tired, Don. I pulled an all-nighter studying for a test I had this morning before I flew out. Had a twelve-page paper due, too. Turned it in early since I knew I'd be here." He exhaled.

I snuggled up next to him, wrapping an arm around his waist. "Thanks for being here, Ash."

"Are you kidding? I wouldn't miss it. When's Corey getting in?"

I inhaled sharply. He turned to face me. "Wait, you still haven't heard from her?"

I didn't answer.

"Well, ok… is she okay? Do you think something's wrong?"

"She's fine. She sent me some short-ass message yesterday saying she'd call me but never did." I stared at the ceiling.

"Oh." He hesitated. "Well, Dev and I struggle with keeping up sometimes, too. Long-distance relationships are—"

"Ash, you just finished telling me how y'all talk all day." I gave him hard side-eye. Still, I appreciated the effort.

"She's got that huge internship. She's probably just over-whelmed."

"Day and night? No way." I paused. "Get this, two girls stopped me in the cafe, asking about Corey like we were friends. One of them bet Corey was enjoying her *new selection* in Cali. Like she did here her first two years."

"Sounds like haters. Probably someone she rejected." He chuckled, then rubbed my arm. "You know she loves you."

I didn't immediately respond.

"All I know is she hasn't been calling me back. And nobody's *that* busy—unless they got someone keeping them busy."

Asher sat up fast, typing on his phone. "Yes! Dev's down. The Down Under tonight."

I groaned. "Ash, I don't feel like it."

"Nope. Saturday's the protest, no time to party then. We're going out." He clapped his hands. "No time for moping."

Before I could argue, he was out the door, towel in hand. I sighed, already regretting the night ahead.

Chapter Twenty

The bass from the music thumped through the pavement as we stepped onto the familiar cobblestone outside *The Down Under*. The night air was crisp, carrying the energy of the city with it. Before we even reached the door, I could feel the vibrations in my chest, the deep pulse of the bar's heartbeat pulling us inside.

Inside, was just as it always was, dark, smoky, and filled with people either dancing, talking close, or sitting at the bar.

Tonight, I decided on black calf-high leather heeled boots, fitted blue jeans, a red turtleneck, and my black leather jacket with silver zippers. Not quite Michael Jackson's "Beat It", but close enough. My hair was pulled into a high curly bun, my makeup light but intentional.

When I walked back into my room before we left, Asher took one look at me and said, "Bitch, you better work! You won't feel lonely for long."

The thought made me feel excited and sad at the same time. Was Corey doing the same somewhere in California? Getting dressed, getting ready, stepping out?

I had never seen Asher wear a mesh shirt before, but his broad frame and height made it work. He paired it with black skinny jeans and all-black Vans.

"What you think?" He posed in the mirror.

I smirked. "I think your body is banging, and Devin is going to love it."

"That's exactly what I'm going for. I think tonight we're going to make love."

I was halfway out the door when I whipped back around. "What did you just say?" My mouth hung open.

"Just because we're two gay boys doesn't mean we're just humping and screwing like jackrabbits." He laughed.

"But you spent almost every night in his room when you were here."

He shrugged, grinning. "The best nights were just talking, getting to know each other."

I twisted my lips. "Mm-hmm."

"Okay, okay! There was lots of touching, passionate kisses, and rubbing, but Dev's a gentleman." His eyes lit up, blinking fast like hummingbird wings.

"Damn it, Asher. You are full of surprises."

* * *

At the bar, I stood with my elbow leaned against the counter, a watered-down drink in my hand, watching Asher and Devin dance like they were trying to outdo each other. Asher moved like he didn't care who was watching, or whether he and the beat agreed. His tall frame commanded attention, his energy pulling people into his orbit.

I chuckled to myself. Watching Asher dance was entertainment all on its own.

"I love that guy. He is so crazy," I mumbled to myself.

"They say it's okay to talk to yourself as long as you don't answer."

I turned to find Alisha smiling widely at me.

"Oh, hey, Alisha." I chuckled, eyes betraying me as they flickered down to her chest. The deep V-neck of her burgundy cashmere sweater left just enough to the imagination. I sipped my drink, trying to focus.

"I wasn't expecting to see you out tonight," she said, arching an eyebrow. "What a pleasant surprise, though." She lifted her drink to her lips, her burgundy lipstick wrapping around the tiny red straw as she sipped.

"I'm surprised to be here myself. Asher's idea." I nodded toward the dance floor.

"Asher's a smart man." She smirked. "Tammy loves DJ RoLinda. She'll have you dancing until you pass out." She bobbed her head to the music, her body naturally moving with the beat.

"Yeah, she's killin' it tonight." I looked around. "Where is Tammy?"

Alisha smiled and shrugged. "Don't know, don't care."

I gave her a *yeah, okay* look, eyeing her up and down. Her thick thighs pressed against green stretch pants, tucked into beige ankle boots, her sweater matching everything perfectly.

Before I could react, she grabbed my hand, pulling me onto the dance floor. "Why are we standing around? Let's dance!"

I barely had time to protest.

* * *

Asher's hands flew up the moment he saw me. "Hey now! I was wondering when you'd get your butt out here!" He spun toward Devin, who was moving with the same reckless joy.

"Sometimes it just takes the right partner to get you out here. Ain't that right, Don?" Alisha's lips curved into a grin.

I felt Asher's eyes zero in on me, squinting with that knowing smirk of his. I quickly looked away, focusing on dancing.

The drink in my system buzzed through me, relaxing my limbs, letting the bass command my body.

I let go.

* * *

After working up a good sweat, I ended up at the bar again, cooling down.

Alisha danced her way over, placing her elbow on the counter next to mine. "What are you drinking?"

I held up my half-empty glass. "H2O."

"Ah. Quitting so soon?" She checked her watch. "It's not even midnight."

I chuckled. "Good. Still time to get home before my outfit turns to rags."

"You'd still be beautiful."

Her words hit me differently than they should have. I shuffled my feet, burying my gaze in my glass as I took another sip.

Alisha leaned toward the bartender. "Two vodka crans."

The bartender, the same one from before, winked at me before pouring the drinks. "You got it."

Alisha slid a twenty onto the counter and pushed a glass toward me. "Cheers."

I hesitated, then clinked my glass against hers.

* * *

A couple more drinks, a few more dances, and the room blurred at the edges. Asher and Devin joined us at the bar. The tequila came next. Salt. Shot. Lime. Another.

Chapter Twenty-One

My eyes pinged open to my dorm room ceiling. My phone vibrated underneath my hip. A dull throb settled behind my eyes, my head pounding in time with my heartbeat. I turned my head, squinting at the screen. Before I could reach for it, my breath caught.

Alisha.

Her soft, bare breast peeked from beneath her lace bra. My stomach flipped, my mind scrambling for details. I searched myself with one hand. Shirt still on—check. Pants still on—check. Unzipped but still on.

I exhaled slowly, rubbing my forehead. What the fuck?

Carefully, I pulled my arm from under Alisha's head. She stirred but didn't wake, her soft snores filling the quiet. I sat up, swallowing past the dryness in my throat. My gaze flickered across the room.

Asher and Devin lay spooned together on a pallet of covers beside me on the floor, fully clothed. Relief flooded through me, but it didn't stop the hammering in my chest. I wiped my face, trying to shake off the fog of last night.

"Oh, God," I grumbled, stumbling in a tiptoe over their tangled limbs. My body swayed as I grabbed my closet door for balance, then reached for a water bottle. I drank it all in one go, the cold liquid doing nothing for the heat creeping up my neck.

A groan sounded behind me. "I think I have a crook."

I turned to find Asher rubbing his neck, his lips smacking dryly before his gaze landed on my bed. "Whoa." His eyebrows shot up, then shifted to me. "What the hell?"

I didn't answer. Just stood there, my mouth suddenly useless.

He shook Devin awake. "Hey, handsome. Let's, um, go to your room."

Devin yawned, rubbing his eyes. "I'm still drunk."

"Mm-hmm, me too." Asher stretched. "Back to sleep?"

Devin nodded. Asher stood, lingering a second too long as his gaze flicked between me and Alisha. "This girl is out."

"All of them damn tequila shots." Devin shook his head before slipping his shoes on.

We stifled quiet laughs, pressing hands to our mouths. Asher walked over, resting a hand on my arm before leaving. "You good?"

I hesitated. "I don't know."

His expression softened, and he gave my arm a squeeze before slipping out the door with Devin.

I turned back to my bed. "Alisha."

Nothing.

I tried again. "Alisha."

She mumbled something, adjusted her pillow, then settled deeper into the covers.

"Fuck." I ran a hand through my hair and glanced at Tiffany's bed, already made. Had she even come home?

My phone vibrated again. I looked down, my stomach knotting at the name on the screen.

Corey.

My heart dropped into my tequila-filled gut as I answered. "Hello? Hello?"

"Hey, Freshy, you asleep?"

"No. Why haven't you called me? I've been calling and texting you." My pulse pounded in my ears.

"I know, I know. I've been crazy busy. I know that's not an excuse, but—"

"Then don't use it. How busy can you be? Too busy to send more than four words in a text? Too busy to just say hello? To call me back?"

"Chandon, baby. I wasn't expecting to be so overwhelmed. It's been intense. I'm just trying to keep up. You know I'm giving it my all…you realize what this means for me. But I miss you like crazy, Freshy. And I can't wait to see you."

My heart softened for a second. "Will you make the protest?"

A pause.

"I—I—uh…"

Silence.

"Hello?" I pulled the phone away, checked the screen, and then pressed it back to my ear. "Are you still there?"

"Y-yeah, I'm here. I couldn't make that happen without falling super behind, Chandon. I tried. But if I miss any of the assigned tasks—"

"What? I'm really not trying to hear that, Corey. You promised me. You said you had your flight and everything. So now what?"

I felt my face heat, the hurt twisting tight inside my chest. The disappointment forced me to sit on my bed.

"I love you so much. I love you so much. I'm going to call more; I'll do better, I promise. I love you. You know that."

I sighed, glancing over at Alisha still asleep beside me. "I—I l-love you, too, Upper." I hesitated. "Corey?"

"Yes?" She sounded like she was smiling.

I swallowed hard. "You not playing me, are you? You're not out there dating other people, are you?"

"What?!" Her voice sharpened. "Hell no! Come on, Freshy!"

"What am I supposed to think? I have to ask. I need to know."

"You supposed to think I'm out here working my ass off trying to do what I came here to do—create change. So no, Freshy. I wouldn't do that to you."

I clenched my teeth. "It's been hella long and now you're saying you're not coming after you told me you were. I need you. I'm texting, calling, leaving voicemails, and you're not even responding. That's not what I'm used to. I knew things would be different, but you said you'd be here to support me, remember?"

Corey exhaled. "I need you, too! I'm so turned on right now just from hearing your voice, even though you're stressing me out. Shit! Give me two more weeks, and I will find a way to get to you."

I clenched my jaw. "The protest will be over."

"Tell me something, Freshy."

"What?" I asked, my voice tight.

"What are you wearing?" Her voice dipped lower, sultry.

A smile crept onto my face despite myself. I missed her too damn much.

"Well," I glanced down at last night's clothes, lowering my voice. "I have on—"

"Don?"

I froze. Alisha sat up beside me, stretching with a yawn.

"I can't believe you awake."

"Who the fuck is that?" Corey snapped.

My eyes widened. I jumped up and pressed a finger to my lips, motioning desperately for Alisha to be quiet.

"Up—Co-Corey, th—that's just Alisha."

"Alisha? What the fuck *she* doing in your room at this time of morning?"

"Corey, please calm down. Me, her, Asher, and Dev...we, um, went out last night." My voice cracked.

"And?"

"And we all came back here and passed out drunk. I don't even remember coming home. I drank too much."

"Put Asher on the goddamn phone."

I winced. "He—he just went back to Devin's room."

"You fucking kidding me right now, Chandon? Alisha? For real? Wow!"

The line clicked. My chest caved in as I stared at the screen.

Alisha stood, pulling on her boots. "You need to figure your shit out."

Then she was gone.

I fell back onto my bed. Tears slid down my temples, soaking into my pillow as I stared at the ceiling, motionless.

BLACK LIVES MATTER
BLACK LIVES MATTER
FREE MONICA & LORRAINE

Chapter Twenty-Two

The day of the protest finally arrived. We'd walked almost two miles from Franklin University to the State Capitol building, which sat high atop the greenest, grassiest hill.

I had visited the location several times before, but as we approached with hundreds of people marching beside and behind us, the weight of it all settled on my chest. It took my breath away.

At the very top of its castle-like dome rested a flagpole, where the state's red, white, and blue flag waved against the sky. Its blue circle at the center enclosed three white stars, one for the middle, west, and east of the state. No one star sat above the others. I found that fact memorable. Poetic, even.

The crowd erupted into chants: "Protect those who protect us! Black Lives Matter! Free Monica and Lorraine!"

Asher and Devin's voices boomed through their megaphones, fiery and relentless as they led the charge. "When I say protect those, you say who protects us! When I say Black Lives, you say Matter! When I say Free, you say Monica and Lorraine!"

Car horns blared in solidarity as we passed intersections. Some drivers raised fists through their windows, honking in rhythm with our chants. Others stopped and stared; phones raised to capture the moment.

And then there were those who barely glanced in our direction, too indifferent or unwilling to acknowledge what was happening.

The weather seemed to be on our side. The sky stretched wide and blue over our heads, soft clouds drifting lazily across it. The sun peeked in and out, warming our skin, but not enough to drain our energy. For once, the world outside felt as if it was rooting for us.

As we neared the Capitol steps, I felt Alisha's hand slip into mine. Her eyes big with anticipation, nerves, excitement. She squeezed my sweaty palm.

"You got this, Don." Her smile was steady, grounding me.

I nodded, inhaled deeply, and climbed the steps to the podium.

With each step, memories flooded through me. My dad putting his life on the line. My mom keeping his absence from swallowing us whole. My grandfather's words ringing in my ears—his warnings, his disappointment, his expectations. The quiet sacrifices. The invisible battles.

And Corey. Her voice had cracked with frustration the day she'd yelled at me on the yard. She needed me to understand—to truly see. But it wasn't just about her anymore. It wasn't about anyone telling me what to see, what to believe, or what to fight for.

The truth had already taken root inside me, spreading through my bones, settling deep into my marrow. For myself and for my family. Both my Black and White family. Black Lives Matter, for all the reasons this country kept telling us they didn't.

From Zora Neale Hurston to my grandparents, to my dad, and for the women who served this country who deserved to be free and brought home.

I gripped the podium as my knees buckled beneath me. My heartbeat thundered in my ears. I opened my mouth, but no words came out.

Shit.

A murmur rippled through the crowd. I felt all the eyes on me, pressing down like a heavy weight, an entire crowd holding its breath in unison. The rustling of signs, the shuffling of feet, the quiet crackle of a megaphone switching on. It all blurred together, amplifying the tightness in my chest.

I could almost hear their thoughts, feel their expectations wrapping around me like invisible hands, pushing me forward or pulling me under. The hush before the storm of voices felt louder than any chant. Waiting. Expecting.

Suddenly, Alisha was beside me. She took my hands in hers, her voice low but firm.

"Don, follow me." She closed her eyes. "Breathe."

I mirrored her, taking in slow, deep breaths. Her presence steadied me, but when her body pressed against mine, a memory from the other night surfaced. Her lips, soft and deliberate, against mine. It wasn't a dream. It was real.

I stepped back up to the mic, heart still thudding in my chest, but this time I let it. I let myself feel everything.

"I—I didn't know what I was going to say when I came up here. Not really. But I do now. A long time ago, I made a promise. I didn't have the words for it back then, and I didn't really understand what it meant. But I do now. It was to my dad. He died overseas working as a military contractor, like Monica Jacobs and Lorraine Cuttleston, the two women we're fighting for today.

He was just trying to give us a better life. He said he'd only be gone a year. He—he never came back.

"So maybe that's why I wear his dog tags every day. Maybe that's why I couldn't stay quiet. Because some promises don't get spoken out loud, they just live inside you. In your chest. In your bones. And maybe this is part of that promise, too. To speak up. To protect people who protect us. To keep going, even when it hurts. Even when you're scared.

"Monica and Lorraine fought for this country. They loved each other, and now they're being punished for it. Locked away. Forgotten. Just like too many others. Black. Queer. Veterans. Human. We can't let that keep happening. Not in silence. So today, I'm keeping that promise. To my father. To Monica and Lorraine. To *myself.* We will not be silent. Not anymore."

The crowd erupted: voices chanting, fists pumping into the sky, signs raised high.

Before I knew it, Asher's arm was around my shoulders, guiding me down the steps and into the crowd.

"You're so fucking amazing!" he shouted above the noise, pulling me into a tight hug.

Tears swelled in my eyes. "Thank you, Asher. I just—I can't believe we did this."

He didn't say anything at first, just smiled, like he knew exactly what this meant to me.

"We did this," I whispered again, like saying it made it real.

"Yes, girl! Believe it."

I turned to see Lisa's bright smile before she wrapped me in an embrace. From the Capitol steps, Chris's voice soared over the crowd. "Free Monica and Lorraine!"

The crowd roared back in unison. Signs waved, fists stayed high, voices rang loud. The energy swelled, pressing against my skin. I was pushed back, but I didn't care. The moment was bigger than me.

Then I saw her.

Corey.

She walked toward me. Her presence was so sudden I blinked, convinced she was a mirage.

"Hey, Freshy." Her voice was calm, steady like she had never been gone.

I threw myself into her arms.

She cupped my face in her hands, her warm palms holding me still before she kissed me—long, deep like she was reclaiming something. My body tightened; my mind went blank.

When she pulled away, she grinned, breathless. "Look at this! Look at you! This is amazing! You were amazing up there, speaking your truth. It was beautiful. I'm so fucking proud of you."

I blinked. "Thanks, Upper. I can't believe you're here!"

She hesitated, then glanced toward the stage. "I saw Alisha up there…" Her voice wavered, throat clearing. "Helping you."

I reached for her hand, but she shoved both of them into her coat pockets.

"Corey, I haven't really talked to you since you left for California. You just…disappeared."

She sighed. "I'm sorry. I wasn't expecting all of this to be so much. So emotional. Bringing up all these feelings inside of me." She looked at me, eyes heavy with longing. "But guess what?"

Her face brightened. "We're working on federal legislation that, if passed, will hold cops accountable for unreasonable use of force. They'll actually be charged with murder."

I opened my mouth to respond, but Alisha appeared, shoving a sign into my hands. "Call it a keepsake," the impatience threading through her voice.

"Thanks, Alisha." I cleared my throat.

"No problem. We're about to march around the building. We ain't done yet!" Her grin was wide, but her gaze flickered to Corey before landing back on me. "You coming?"

I hesitated. My chest tightened.

"Do you mind giving us a moment?" Corey's voice was clipped.

Alisha scoffed. "Surprised you're even here right now."

Corey stepped forward. Face to face. Eye to eye. I moved between them, pulse hammering. "Alisha—"

"Don, I'll be waiting after the march. Don't leave me."

She reached for my hand. I swallowed hard, my throat suddenly dry. Our fingers barely lingered against each other's.

"Ms. MIA," she mumbled before walking away.

I turned back to Corey. She just stared back at me.

"Alisha, huh?" Her voice was light, but her eyes weren't. "Or should I say 'Lish'?"

I had no response.

It started like a ripple, murmurs that turned into confusion, confusion that escalated into alarm. The steady rising of voices clashed against the chants of the protest, a jagged disruption that sliced through the unity of the crowd. A wall of red began moving toward us, parting the sea of people like a force of nature.

A swarm of red-robed figures surged forward, their movements rehearsed and aggressive. Signs, massive wooden crosses, and banners painted with Bible verses in dripping black ink. Their voices were a unified wail of condemnation, their words sharp as blades.

"Abomination!"

"God's wrath is upon you!"

"Sin leads to hell!" The air thickened, crackling with their fury.

"Repent! Homosexuality is an abomination! Repent!"

I grabbed Corey's hand. Her grip tightened instantly, her knuckles white. "We need to go. Now."

My heart slammed against my ribs as the mob pressed in, their bodies like a tide threatening to sweep us under. At first, they were just a distant rumble of voices, like thunder before a storm breaks.

Then the red sea parted the crowd, flowing toward us with purpose. Red robes, red faces, red signs. The air around us changed. Thick and charged like before a lightning strike. People near me tensed, their bodies stiffening as conversations halted mid-sentence.

From the corner of my eye, I caught fleeting movements: some protesters backing away, others pressing forward with defiant stances, phones raised high to capture whatever came next.

The robed figures moved with the synchronized precision of pillagers, their voices growing from murmurs into a wall of sound that crashed against our chants. Their signs bobbed above the crowd, wooden crosses and Bible verses dripping with red paint-like blood. Every hair on my arms stood on end.

I clutched Corey's hand tighter, feeling her pulse race against mine. The air tasted metallic, the scent of sweat and fear and rage mixing into something primal. Even the sun seemed to dim as shadows stretched between us and them, the space shrinking with each passing second.

Before we could move, I saw him. A man at the center of it all, clad in a red, white, and blue preacher's robe, his arms raised high like some self-appointed prophet of destruction. His eyes locked onto me, wild with something unhinged. He wasn't just shouting, he was charging. His gaze burned with hatred so pure it froze me in place.

Recognition flickered across his face, like he'd found what he was looking for. Something in the way he moved toward me, parting the crowd with his body, made my throat close up. A voice in my head screamed *Run*, but my feet wouldn't listen.

His arm lifted. A glint of silver, the unmistakable shine of metal catching the sunlight. Time slowed, my breath catching in my throat as the object in his hand became clear.

"Repent!" he roared, his voice like a crack of thunder, his eyes alight with something terrifyingly resolute.

Corey's scream shattered through the chaos, visceral and raw. I barely had time to react before the world tilted. A shove. The rush of air. The ground rising to meet me. Then—darkness.

Chapter Twenty-Three

"Broken arm, bruised ribs, lacerated and swollen lip. She also has a concussion. The good news is that we expect a full recovery. Help her to rest up, keep her stress levels down, and make sure she drinks plenty of water."

The voices drifted through my foggy consciousness, muffled and distant at first, then sharpening as I blinked awake. The shapes became clearer. Faces hovering over me, hands clutching mine. A white coat came into focus. Brown skin, thick black hair pulled back, dark eyes scanning a clipboard.

A doctor.

I tried to sit up, but pain exploded through my skull, a dull throb spreading behind my eyes. I groaned.

"It's okay, baby. Mommy is here."

Warm tears slid down my temples as my mother's voice wrapped around me. Her hand rested gently on my shoulder, her lips pressing soft and firm against my cheek. "Your grandfather and grandmother are here, too, baby girl."

I turned my head and saw them. My grandparents, standing close by, and my aunt Ronda was beside them. I looked back toward my mom, her eyes swollen and glassy, and then I saw him—E.J. My brother, standing next to her, arms crossed, a half smirk across his lips.

"Who gets knocked out at their own protest, genius?" he muttered, shaking his head.

A weak chuckle slipped out before the pain smothered it back down.

"E.J.," my mother warned.

"Young man, step into the hallway. Now is not the time for that," my grandfather chastised him.

E.J. scoffed but obeyed, slipping out the door. A small pang of disappointment settled in my chest. As much as he got on my nerves, I wanted him nearby. I wanted to hear his voice—his teasing, his way of making the worst moments seem a little less unbearable. But he was gone, and the room felt emptier without him. My mother glared at my grandfather, but before she could say anything, I tried to push myself up again.

That's when I noticed the man in the corner. Broad shoulders. Tall. Brown hair buzzed close to his scalp. A neatly trimmed goatee. His tan skin, his stiff posture, everything about him felt out of place in this room.

"Who is that?" I groaned.

My mom's hand pressed against my chest, urging me back down. "Relax, baby. Relax."

"Your mother thought it was a good idea to bring her—" my grandfather started.

My grandmother nudged his arm sharply with her elbow. "Now is not the time, like you just told E.J." She turned to me, her voice softening.

"How you feel, baby?" Her smile was warm and familiar, the kind that smelled like Sunday morning biscuits or warm apple pie.

"That's Carl, Donny. He is my friend." My mother's voice was low and steady.

Friend. Right, I thought.

The doctor cleared her throat. "You're here for the night, Chandon. We expect a release sometime tomorrow. Rest up. Dinner will be here shortly—meatloaf. Buzz the nurse if you need anything."

"Thank you, Dr. Singh," my mother said as the doctor left the room.

Silence stretched between us for only a second before my grandfather's voice cut through it.

"Don, I told you to go to Franklin and become a leader, not a troublemaker."

My aunt Ronda's head popped up. "Good trouble." She winked at me, her smile playful.

"Donny is not a troublemaker, Emanuel. If anything, you're the one who put her up to this," my mom shot back at him.

I had never heard my mother speak to my grandfather like that. Her voice was tight, sharp.

"I'm just making sure my grandbaby knows who she is. Which is more than I can say for you." His tone was even, but the weight behind his words made my mother's cheeks flush red.

I saw the tears brimming in her hazel eyes before she blinked them away. Before I could say anything, Carl was at her side, his arm slipping around her shoulder.

"Trying to raise a White woman, that's what!" My grandfather's voice rose, the anger cracking through.

"Dad. Don't." My aunt Ronda's voice was firm but pleading.

"Granddad," I said, my voice steadier than I expected. "Dad chose both worlds—Black and White. That's who I am. That's not Mom's fault. It's dad's gift to me and E.J. If you don't see that, you don't see me, you don't see us." I felt a warm tear slip from my eye and streak down the side of my face.

My mom gently caressed my head.

"Your son loved me, and I loved him. All of him, Emanuel," my mother said quietly. "Not just the parts that fit your expectations."

"You cannot stand here and tell me my son would have been okay with how you're raising his children! A homosexual. A homosexual White woman at that! I said civil rights activist. Not some pro-homosexual activist." He spat the word *homosexual* out his mouth like it was two separate insulting words, both equally vile.

Before anyone could respond, the door swung open, and two nurses stepped inside.

"Alright, everyone," the older nurse said, her voice calm but commanding. "We're going to need you all to step out to the waiting room."

They didn't argue. One by one, they left, the air still crackling from the tension they left behind.

Finally, silence.

I exhaled shakily, my body sinking deeper into the mattress. The quiet gave me space to think—to remember. The preacher. His outstretched arm. The flash of metal. Corey's scream.

I looked down at my right arm, heavy in a cast. My busted lip still stung, the taste of dried blood lingering on my tongue.

But what about Monica and Lorraine? Were they still unlawfully detained in Kuwait?

The door creaked open again. I turned my head slowly, and there they were. Alisha, Corey, Devin, and Asher.

They moved cautiously like their very footsteps might break me.

"Chandon, dear. You have some visitors." A nurse walked in behind them, adjusting the monitoring machines before pressing a button that lifted my bed upright. "I'm so glad you have friends here. It helps." She smiled. "Let me know if you need anything."

Asher was the first to step forward. He hesitated before running his fingers over my cast.

"It was still a success," he whispered. His eyes were worried, searching. "I'm going to be the first one to sign this."

I winced, smirking slightly. "You know I'm going to fully recover, right?"

He sighed but nodded, stepping aside as Alisha and Corey moved to either side of me. Alisha placed a small, round glass vase of fresh flowers on the nightstand next to the water pitcher. The bouquet was a mix of wildflowers, deep purple asters, soft yellow daisies, and tiny blue forget-me-nots. The colors clashed yet somehow blended perfectly together, vibrant and full of life.

Seeing them there, bright against the sterile white of the hospital room, spread warmth through my aching body. I turned to Alisha, my lips curling into a small, grateful smile.

Out of the corner of my eye, I caught Corey's reaction, her jaw tightening, the muscle flickering beneath her skin. Her fingers, which had just moments ago held mine with care, twitched slightly before curling into a loose fist.

She forced a small, tight-lipped smile, but the heat in her eyes betrayed her. It wasn't just irritation—it was something deeper, something almost resentful.

"Don, I'm right here, hon." Alisha grabbed my hand, squeezing gently.

Corey reached for my other hand, the one wrapped in the cast and held it more firmly. Her grip tightening, not enough to hurt but enough to remind me she was there. Her hand traced over my arm with care, but there was tension behind it, something unspoken simmering just beneath the surface.

Their eyes locked. The tension was instant.

Corey's voice was firm. "Well, thanks for checking on your *friend*. You can go now."

Alisha rolled her eyes. "Look, can I have a moment alone with her, please?"

Corey shook her head, her voice calm but clipped. "Hell no…never again. Chandon is *my* woman. I heard you've been confused about that."

Alisha's jaw clenched. "Actions speak louder than words, so I'm not confused about anything."

The nurse returned at that moment, exhaling as she crossed her arms. "We can't have this in here. Ms. Kilpatrick needs rest, not a tug-of-war. I'm sorry."

Another nurse, a tall, broad-shouldered man stepped in. His arms folded over his chest. "Do we need to call security?"

Corey scoffed. "Great. Look what you did." She kissed me soft on my bruised lips. "Don, I'm going to step out, but I'll be back. I love you." She glared at Alisha before she walked out.

The door clicked shut behind Corey, leaving the room quiet except for the beeping machines. My heart pounded against my bruised ribs. Damn. I was literally caught in a hospital bed with no escape, stuck between two women who were ready to throw down over me while I couldn't even sit up straight.

I closed my eyes and took a deep breath, but all I saw were their faces. Corey all jealous and pissed, Alisha, standing her ground like she was marking territory. The pain meds helped the physical aches, but they did nothing for the ones spreading through my heart. When I opened my eyes again, Alisha was still there, staring at me with a look that made my breath catch in my throat.

She stepped closer. "Don..."

Her face looked different now. That fire in her eyes when she was going at it with Corey—gone. In its place was something soft, something that made me nervous in a whole different way.

As I lay there looking at her, it hit me how far we'd come since that day she called me out for dissing her when Corey showed up. All those times Alisha had my back when Corey was MIA in California.

Even with the meds making my thoughts all fuzzy and confusing, I knew whatever came out of her mouth next was gonna change everything between us.

I met her eyes. "It's not your fault, Lish. I'll be fine. I check out tomorrow." I assured her.

She bent closer, her breath warm against my ear. "Good, because…I think I might love you."

* * *

The next morning, I woke to find Tiffany sitting in the chair beside my bed, her textbook open on her lap. She looked up, startled like she wasn't expecting me to catch her there.

"How long you been sitting there?" I asked, my voice still groggy with sleep.

She closed her book and sat up straighter. "Not long. I had an 8 AM lab across the street."

I raised my eyebrows. "So, you just decided to pop in and watch me sleep?"

"I saw the video," she said abruptly. "Of you getting hit. It's everywhere."

I shifted in the bed, wincing as pain shot through my ribs. "Yeah? I'm famous now, huh?"

"Famous for the wrong reasons, if you ask me." The familiar judgment crept into her voice, but then she paused, her eyes dropping to my cast. "But I shouldn't have said what I said before. About you wasting your time."

"Oh?" This was new.

"My dad was in Desert Storm," she said quietly. "He never talks about it, but I know it messed him up. My mom said nobody was protesting for veterans' rights when he came back with PTSD , and he had to fight with the VA to diagnose him properly."

She pulled something from her bag and placed it on my bedside table. A protein bar and a small bottle of vitamin water.

"You need to eat better if you're going to heal. Hospital food is garbage." She stood up, slinging her bag over her shoulder. "Anyway, I put in a maintenance request to get your bed adjusted before you come back. The angle will be better for your arm and bruises."

"Thanks, Tiffany."

She nodded once, already halfway to the door. "Don't thank me. Thank my mom."

I smiled as the door closed behind her. Maybe we didn't have to be friends, but it seemed like we could be roommates after all.

Chapter Twenty-Four

The protest made national news after all, but not for the right reasons. A video of me being attacked and knocked unconscious went viral across social media and news networks.

As I watched the footage, I saw Corey scream for help, never leaving my side. My heart still raced every time I saw it, like I was right back there, reliving the chaos.

What I hadn't remembered—since I was already unconscious—was being trampled by panicked people as some of the red-hooded terrorists pulled out AR-15s. First came sadness, then anger, then rage.

The man who'd proclaimed to be rebuking Satan from me turned out to be a preacher. He'd been arrested.

My grandfather, Aunt Ronda, and Uncle Dee said they'd make sure he was charged and sentenced for assaulting me. I had no doubt they would.

The footage stirred something in the public. Two of our state's representatives released statements calling for an investigation into Monica and Lorraine's case. A hashtag trended: #freemonicaandlorraine. It wasn't everything we'd hoped for, they were still imprisoned in Kuwait, but it was something. A crack in the wall of silence. Dad would've been proud.

* * *

I'd been out of the hospital for almost a month. My arm was still in its cast, and the bruising had nearly faded. All kinds of people I didn't know stopped me as I walked around campus, offering words of encouragement and admiration for the protest. Some even apologized for their treatment of me earlier in the year.

Whatever. I wasn't quick to forgive people who had ruined the start of my freshman year with hateful rumors. Still, I was grateful. The way I was treated had lit a fire under me. It pushed me out of my comfort zone.

My reputation had changed, though. Invitations poured in from nearly every club and organization on campus, asking me to join or speak at their meetings and events. I declined. I didn't want to be anyone's five-minute celebrity.

* * *

It was one of those days when the weather began teasing us with change. The morning had been frigid, but the warmth of the afternoon melted it away. My sweater was tied around my waist as I walked, my headphones stuffed in my ears to avoid conversation.

Walking toward Nash-Jamison Hall hadn't lost its magic for me. Its presence was as commanding as ever, and I didn't know if I'd ever grow used to it. The brick arches, the towering windows, the way sunlight cast long shadows across its entrance, it was more than a building. It was history itself. I found myself staring, lost in thought until my view was interrupted.

A tall figure stepped into my path, a large, round Afro catching the afternoon light, silver bangles jingling with each movement. Dr. Collier was headed straight for me.

"Ms. Kilpatrick. I see you have found your voice."

I stopped in my tracks.

"Dr. Collier, how are you?" I fiddled with the sleeves of my sweater.

"Alive and well. I'm certainly glad to hear the same is true of you." She nodded. "I'm proud of you."

I looked up, slightly startled.

"Don't be surprised. You are among the few students who arrive on Franklin's hallowed grounds already cultivated, already sprouting." She gestured wide with her arms like a rainbow. "A bit of water, and pow! First bloom. Thirty years of teaching will do that. You learn to recognize the ones who come in ready to bloom immediately."

I gave a nervous nod and grin.

"Don't worry, I won't keep you too long." She studied my face. "That isn't to say you don't have much to learn, much room to grow. No, it simply means your soil is rich and fertilized. The seeds have been planted and tended to. How marvelous! Everyone comes in at their own stages of growth. No stage is better than another. Do you understand?"

I nodded again, but I wasn't sure I fully grasped what she meant.

"You are powerful, Chandon." She tapped my shoulder with each word. The jingling of her bangles rang in the space between us. "Don't be fooled. *The most common way people give up their power is by thinking they don't have any.* Do you know who said that?"

I hesitated, looking around as if the answer might be floating in the air. "No, I don't."

"Alice Walker, my dear." She lingered on my reaction before continuing. "And what is the connection between Alice Walker and Zora Neale Hurston?"

I didn't know, but I placed my hand on my chin and pretended to ponder her question. Dr. Collier laughed at me.

"Take my Black Women in American Literature class when you return in the fall. I expect to see you enrolled soon. Think about what Ms. Walker means by that and be prepared to share your thoughts in class."

"Thank you, Dr. Collier." My response carried more confidence than before.

"No. Thank *you*. Enjoy the rest of this beautiful day." She continued on her way, leaving me standing there.

I sighed, shaking my head. How did I end up with homework for a class I hadn't even registered for yet? Only at Franklin.

* * *

Back in my room, I lay on my bed, staring at the ceiling. The smooth, off-white surface became a projector screen for my thoughts.

I folded my arms behind my head. The hard cast pressed against the back of my skull, a physical reminder of the hate masquerading as righteousness in this world.

Tiffany sat at her desk, completely immersed in her studying. Her headphones were in, her eyes scanning her notes with laser focus. I admired her dedication. Since the protest, she had spent more time in our room, checking in on me more often.

Besides Alisha, she had been the most attentive, bringing me food from the café and helping me study when I wasn't ready to return to class but needed to keep up.

She was honest, too. She didn't agree with how much time I spent outside of class on non-academic activities, but she respected me for it. And I admitted that I respected her for staying focused on her goals despite the distractions and pressures of college life.

My phone chimed. I had forgotten to set it to vibrate.

Tiffany turned and shushed me. "Can you please put that thing on vibrate? I have a huge chem exam tomorrow."

"Sorry!" I flipped the tiny lever on the side and looked at my phone.

I miss you. It was a text from Corey.

The last time we'd been together flashed across my mind as if the ceiling had become a movie screen. My face was wet with tears as if the moment had just happened all over again. I wiped them away quickly and glanced at Tiffany. She was still focused on her books, oblivious.

I exhaled and placed my phone beside me. A knock at my door made me jump. I rolled off the bed and opened it.

Alisha stood in the doorway, her head tilted slightly, her lips curled into that easy smile of hers. "You gon' stay hidden in this room forever?"

I chuckled. "Maybe." My voice heavy with honesty.

Her smile widened. "I don't think so. Come take this walk with me." Her eyes were bright, filled with something promising. Something I hadn't felt in weeks.

She smiled and reached for my hand.

World
Famous
Griller

Epilogue

The Midwest's summer heat shimmered above the grill; its familiar thick humidity clung to my skin as I led Alisha through the fence into my grandfather's backyard. We'd been home for the summer for two weeks, and the freedom and mental clarity that June brought to me was exactly what I needed after the year I had.

I played around with the idea of going to summer school but agreed with my mom that I had done more than enough during my first year of college to have earned a break. The familiar scents of charcoal and my grandfather's secret BBQ sauce wrapped around me like a welcome home hug.

"So, this is the famous Mr. Emanuel Kilpatrick's cookout. It looks just like you described it," Alisha said, her eyes widening at the sprawling yard filled with my relatives.

Her shoulder brushed against mine, a touch that still sent sensual currents through me despite our carefully negotiated "just friends" agreement we'd decided on last month.

It was clear that Alisha didn't want me talking to Corey anymore and I wasn't going to stop despite me saying I would. It was also clear that Corey and I had unresolved feelings that weren't going anywhere, no matter how far apart we were.

We hadn't officially broken up, but we weren't together either. We were a...gray area. The distance had changed us, but neither of us was willing to let go.

Alisha and I spent the last few weeks of the spring semester toeing the line. Lingering touches, soft kisses that deepened before we caught ourselves, moments where clothes shifted but stayed on.

We hadn't had sex, but we came close more than once. It felt natural, almost inevitable, and harder to stop each time.

She had been there for me all year, but after the protest and the attack, her loyalty became something else—steadfast, protective. She made sure I stayed on top of my classes, helped me push through finals, reminded me to eat, to sleep. She didn't just show up, she stood beside me. And I loved her for that.

But in between it all, Corey called and texted me every day and each time, I answered. My feelings for Alisha were real and true. But they were still strong for Corey, too. And I couldn't deny that. I didn't want to, either.

Alisha didn't *exactly* force me to choose her, but she let her feelings be known. She wasn't playing second fiddle to anyone. Our friendship and being in each other's lives meant more to us, we both agreed.

But the agreement hadn't erased the tension that hummed between us like a plucked guitar string whenever we were alone together. I didn't tell Corey I was bringing Alisha with me to my grandfather's house.

To be fair, I didn't tell her Asher would be coming through either. I convinced myself she didn't need to know everything I was doing. Hell, I didn't know everything she was doing in California. Besides, it seemed like a good idea at the time.

"Baby girl!" My grandfather spotted us from his post at the grill and waved a spatula in greeting. We walked up to the porch where he stood, with his famous apron on, ready to interrogate the witness, I thought. "And this must be your *friend* from school."

The way he emphasized "friend" let me know he was still trying to adjust to his new understanding of who I was, that he was still grappling with my sexuality. I pushed past it. That was his issue, not mine. I felt Alisha stiffen slightly beside me before her instinctive poise kicked in and she extended her hand.

"I'm Alisha. Thank you for having me, Mr. Kilpatrick. Your home is beautiful."

As my grandfather launched into his standard welcome speech and list of questions, my attention drifted over to the card table where Aunt Ronda and Uncle Dee sat. I knew if they weren't already, they were about to engage in a heavy debate.

Last week, when I stopped by, the topic that dominated our family conversations was unarmed Black people being killed by police. My grandfather had gotten so upset it seemed to be carving canyons of grief into his heart. Each new headline another erosion of his hope.

In the year prior, the names had fallen like heavy stones into our family conversations: Eric Garner, Sandra Bland, Michael Brown, Tamir Rice. The bitter taste of injustice lingered after each discussion, as predictable as the seasons: no charges, no crimes, just unarmed Black women and men killed.

"Dead. Murdered," my grandfather would seethe, his voice like rolling thunder across the sky.

I felt Alisha shift beside me on the lawn chair, our fingers accidentally touching on the armrest like a spark jumping between live wires.

"Your family is intense," she whispered, leaning over towards me, her breath warm against my ear, sending a charged current down my spine. "I love it."

I smiled, trying to ignore how the late afternoon sunlight caught the amber flecks in her brown eyes. "Just wait until they really get going."

We settled in to watch the spades game, where my Aunt Ronda held court. The older I got, the more experiences I began to have, the more I admired her. She never backed down from my grandfather or uncle, her words precise as a surgeon's blade, cutting through arguments with the ease of someone who had honed her intellect to a razor's edge.

She was cool and easy, like a breeze sneaking through an open window on a sweltering day. When I finally told her about Stephanie, she simply asked, without hesitation, "Is she cute?" with a chuckle that sounded like two sisters sharing a secret.

Aunt Ronda was my go-to, no question. I wanted to be like her. Everything about her — smart, successful, strong — pulled me in. She and my grandmother were the only two who never seemed to shrink around my grandfather. Whenever I was with her, I was like a sponge, soaking it all up. As she organized the cards in her hand with practiced precision, I watched that same strength in action.

"There is no such thing as Black-on-Black violence, Dee. That's just terminology used to divert our attention away from systemic racism and White supremacy," my aunt Ronda said while slamming a playing card on the square card table.

The sound cracked like a small thunderclap in the summer air. She always sat directly across from my uncle, their partnership at the spades table as reliable as the sunrise, even though their ideological battles raged with the intensity of summer thunderstorms.

"Damn, Chandon," Alisha whispered, leaning even closer. "You didn't tell me your aunt was this fierce. And—and beautiful." She bit her lower lip, eyes fixed on my aunt.

Something sharp and unexpected twisted in my stomach. A serpent of jealousy I hadn't prepared myself for. I forced a reserved shrug. "She's almost forty, Lish."

"And aging like fine wine," Alisha replied with a nod and smirk that made my cheeks flush hot.

I marveled at how, when the dust of their arguments settled, my aunt and uncle got up from the table, slapping hands and laughing, their earlier tension fading like steam off a pot left to cool.

My grandfather presided over it all, his "World Famous Griller" red apron a battle flag against the backdrop of his domain. Each time he lifted the hood of his black, rusty metal, Weber grill, tendrils of gray charcoaled smoke spiraled skyward like prayers, carrying the aroma of well-seasoned meats into the crystal-blue canopy above.

The scent wove its way through the yard, an invisible thread stitching us all together, making mouths water in anticipation. Pride bloomed across his face like the unfurling petals of a flower, his laughter harmonizing with my grandmother's as they stood sentinel on the redwood patio deck, surveying their kingdom.

My little cousins ran around like hummingbirds, their laughter a sweet backdrop to the intense discussions of the adults. Dominoes and bid whist games unfolded at tables scattered across the yard like islands in a green sea, but nothing rivaled the connected picnic tables that was the heartbeat of the gathering.

All kinds of covered dishes were organized on them, all strategically placed by my grandmother beneath the ancient oak tree whose branches spread like protective arms, offering shade, beauty, and adventure for my cousins.

The whole family scene played out across the massive backyard's freshly cut grass that felt cool against bare feet. Basically my grandparents' own little kingdom where they presided over everything.

"No such thing, huh?" My uncle Daniel's voice cut through my reverie. "When was the last time you were in the 'hood, little sister? These dudes are out there killing folks like it's a GTA video game." He sipped from his red plastic cup, the liquid inside catching the sunlight like amber.

"You ain't lying," added my cousin Maine from his left. One more cousin on my father's side of the family, too numerous to track.

"I mean, there's truth to that," I said, surprising myself with my own voice. I was usually a quiet sideline guest in these debates, absorbing it all while looking for points to use when debating my grandfather.

But something about Alisha's presence beside me, perhaps wanting to impress her, or maybe just the newfound courage and leader I'd become at Franklin, pushed me forward.

Aunt Ronda turned slightly, her eyebrow-raised at my interjection.

"See!" Uncle Dee pointed triumphantly in my direction. "The young folks know what's up."

"But," I continued, finding my voice growing stronger, "it's also true that the media covers those shootings differently than when cops kill unarmed Black people."

Alisha gently leaned into me, a gesture of support that sent warmth flooding through me.

"At my high school," she added, "we had a White kid bring a gun to school, and they called it a 'mental health incident.' If it had been one of us..." She let the implication hang in the air.

Aunt Ronda nodded approvingly. "Exactly. We got to start asking ourselves questions about how we got here, big brother," she said, injecting the familial title with a honey-sweet mockery.

"How did we get here? Let's see, people's socio-economic status begets crime because folks in poverty commit crimes of survival. History has shown us that systems of racism have continually underfunded Black schools before and after segregation.

"Underfunded schools lead to undereducated people, dropouts, poor trade skills, crime, prison, and then a struggle to acclimate back into society because who wants to hire an ex-con, right?" She slammed another card on the table, the sound like a punctuation mark at the end of her soliloquy. "It's systemic. It's intentional."

"Your aunt is incredible," Alisha whispered, her eyes wide with admiration. "Does she teach somewhere? I would take her class in a heartbeat."

"She's a public defender," I murmured back, trying not to let my annoyance show. "And yeah, she *is* brilliant."

"That's our book!" Aunt Ronda barked at my cousin Tony, whose hand crept like ivy toward the discard pile. She snatched up the cards just before his heist could succeed, stacking them beside her with a flourish that announced her territorial claim.

"Nice. I was hoping you wouldn't cut me out," my uncle winked at her, his eyes twinkling with mischief. "But I hear what you're saying, Ronda. And—and, you know what I'm tired of? All these damn excuses. The fact is, we Black! Life is going to be harder for us. Since we know that, we have to play the game to win. The shit ain't no secret!"

Both Tony and Maine nodded their heads in agreement like they'd been listening to the same beat.

"It's hard to play to win when the rules change as soon as progress is made," she said, her words unfolding slow and sure, like smoke rising off a backyard grill.

"You know what? You need to slow down on the yack 'cause your argument is full of more holes than a pair of daddy's old socks, my brother." Her smile eased across her face, like morning glories opening to the sun.

"She married, huh? I bet she is," Alisha breathed, barely audible.

"Yeah," I lied, the words escaping before I could stop them. Aunt Ronda had been divorced for three years.

Alisha's face fell. "Damn."

A small, mean satisfaction bloomed in my chest.

"I got you. But check this out," Uncle Dee continued. "Look at our parents. Look at us. How are some Black people able to succeed and others aren't? It's about willpower and perseverance.

"And I don't need to slow down at all. It's actually helping me play better," he took another sip, winked at her, and threw down a card with the confidence of a man placing his bet on a sure thing.

"There will always be exceptions to the rule," Aunt Ronda countered. She glanced in my direction, and for a heart-stopping moment, I thought she might have overheard my lie. But she just at me smiled, a look of pride passing over her face.

"But daddy talks to us about the racism he experienced in the military, in the south while attending undergrad, in law school in D.C., and how he was blackballed from making partner at two different law firms before he and Uncle Richard started their own."

Her words gathered momentum like a summer storm. "There aren't too many Black men coming out of law school going to work for their daddy, Dee. Count yourself lucky and check your privilege. Black people aren't killing other Black people because they're Black. But that is exactly what is happening when White cops kill unarmed Black folk.

"Crime is about proximity, and neighborhoods across America continue to be segregated. When murders and crime happen, it's largely by someone of the same race. So, why don't we hear about White-on-White crime?" She folded her arms across her chest.

"Because when was the last drive-by in a White community that killed innocent babies and shit?" he scoffed, his words sharp and steady.

"Jesus, Dee. These motherfuckers are pure, devout terrorists running up in schools, movie theaters, and churches, killing everyone in sight—babies included!" Her voice rose like a tide.

"You right about that," he mumbled, retreating momentarily behind his cup.

"We grew up learning about the Columbine shooting and dealing with the consequences of it," I said, finding courage in Alisha's approving glance. "And we're still having mass shootings at schools. That seems like terrorism to me."

"Exactly, baby girl." Aunt Ronda nodded at me, and I felt a rush of pride at her acknowledgment. "Why aren't we profiling White men? Why don't the media talk about White men as terrorists? The fact is, Black Lives Matter and other movements do a lot of community work to alleviate crime within the Black community, but it isn't talked about. *We* got to be better about not believing the racial stereotypes amplified in all forms of media to justify the murders of Black people by crooked, racist cops."

"Damn, sis. You a public defender of the highest order, huh?" Uncle Daniel leaned forward, examining the final four cards in his hand like a general planning his last stand.

"I think I'mma go to law school after undergrad," Alisha announced suddenly. "Maybe become a public defender like your aunt." Her eyes remained fixed on my aunt, a look of naked admiration on her face.

Aunt Ronda rose from her chair and, with the dramatic flair of a stage performer, slammed down her remaining cards one by one. Each card hit the table with the finality of a judge's gavel, scattering across the grass like leaves in the wind.

With each theatrical slam, she punctuated the air: "Yes...I... am...dammit! And that's game!"

"Bullshit," my cousin Maine groaned, his head shaking like a pendulum as he and Tony surrendered their remaining cards to the table.

Uncle Dee stood, and even after all the back-and-forth, they slapped hands in that same old handshake, like always. That was just how they were. A tight bond, the kind that made me think of me and E.J.

"You would've taken another 'L' today if you weren't my partner, bro. And if daddy was listening, he'd be so disappointed in you. Here, read this book, Daniel," she teased, her voice dropping to a comical baritone.

Uncle Dee laughed, his gaze drifting toward my grandfather like a compass finding north. "I'm my own man with my own thoughts."

"Mm-hmm," was all she said, that note of doubt hanging in the air between them. They walked toward the picnic tables loaded with food.

"Come on," I said to Alisha. "Let's get some food before it's all gone."

As we walked toward the tables, Alisha whispered, "So, your aunt seems cool. Maybe you could introduce me properly?"

"You're kidding, right?"

Alisha shrugged. "I just want to pick her brain about law school. Maybe she can be my mentor."

I chuckled. "Let's just enjoy the food. My grandfather can throw down on the grill. And wait 'til you taste my grandmother's cooking!"

Alisha nodded, her shoulder brushing against mine as we walked. Her touch sending another familiar exhilarating jolt through me, complicated by the jealousy bubbling just under the surface.

I tried to shake it off, tried to focus on the happiness around us instead. But it crept in anyway, the way thoughts always did when you weren't paying attention.

Just like at my grandfather's house, I had seen it at Franklin too. Some of us shouted "Black Lives Matter!" while others had pushed back. "Black lives gotta matter to Black people first."

But watching my family, how they could argue loud and love harder, I started to think maybe the truth wasn't in one side or the other. Maybe it lived somewhere in the messy middle, where hard conversations didn't tear you apart, they brought you closer.

Maybe that was where Alisha and I belonged too. Not in fear, not in jealousy. But maybe in that messy middle. The place where you were scared but showed up anyway.

Was I even capable of being just her friend? Really? Because it didn't feel like it. She was busy admiring my aunt, and I was acting like a green-eyed fool. What would I do when it was somebody she actually had a shot with? Could I handle that?

Was I keeping her close to block her from finding somebody else? No. That wasn't it. I didn't think so anyway.

As we filled our plates under the sprawling oak tree, I made myself a promise: before the summer was over, I was going to figure it out. I wasn't going to run from it. Some games, you played to win.

Rainbow Peeps & Friends, Taylor & Melony are back! Don't want spoilers? Pick up a copy of Rainbow today, then come back and scan the QR code to keep reading! Enjoy!

Taylor & Melony: Ten Years Later

Scan to read!

Acknowledgements

"If you want to go fast, go alone. If you want to go far, go together." -African Proverb

First, thank you God! Thank you, in all things, always. I am created by God; therefore, God is in me, and I am connected to the universe, the heavens and the earth, which have all been created by God. It is the true circle of life. I am grateful for this understanding. Ase. Amen.

Thank you to my ancestors who are my angels. They guide me, they protect me in ways I cannot imagine, they are the force that pushes me every single day. They remind me of who I am and from whence I have come. And when I forget, they whisper to my heart and remind me of why I am here. I am grateful for this connection and understanding.

To one of my newest and greatest ancestors: my big brother James E. Green (Bro!). Thank you for: Every. Single. Thing. The sacrifices you made for your family are immeasurable. I miss you in ways that can only be expressed in tears, smiles, laughs, silences, and thoughts. This book, and every single one I write going forward, is dedicated to you in spirit. I hope I continue to make you proud.

To my favorite girl, mama. You'll always be my favorite girl. You are a true manifestation of God's love on earth, and I am so glad you chose to bring me into this world. In the words of one of your favorite artists, Tina Turner, "you're simply the best!"

To my brother and sister, Michele and Sterling (NB); thank you for your love and prayers. Thank you for reading my work and believing in me. Thank you to my big sis-in-love, Tanya "GF" All Day Every Day! (LOL)

Thank you to my father, Adolfo C. Arzu, we were born on the same day years apart but with the same no-quit, Capricorn spirit of determination and resistance. Thank you for all those lectures on education as a tool of freedom. I hated them then, but I covet and repeat them now. #priceless

Thank you to Ruby "Scooby" Harden. We been doing this thang since you thought you was *all* that freshmen year back in High School! It's a beautiful thing to have someone know me and love me for that long! You know where the bodies are buried. 👀

Thank you to Ebony ("Big Eb"), Bianca & Henley (family), Margaret (my ridah) #HarrietTubman, Mariah (Writing Warrior), Mallory (Writing Warrior), Katie (Writing Warrior), Mary (one of my first beta readers), Kachiside of Make-It-Madu Images for the fly ass back cover photo! John (my amazing barber). I miss those cuts, man! David, Shanae, Sherry (RiRi), and Darryl for reading my work and supporting me!

Thank you to my cuzzos who continue to support, believe, and love me just as I am. Stacie, Qawana (Nana), and Judy Ann Berry. I love y'all, joe! Thank you to Auntie Nita. Thank you for acknowledging the fact that your niece is a published author even if you don't agree with all that I write! I appreciate you for that.

Thank you to Michelle Gilford for your time and consultations surrounding character authenticity. Chandon is better because of you.

Thank you all for your love, support, encouragement, and belief. I am blessed to know and have you all in my life!

To my uncle **Maine**. We miss you, your jokes, your laughter, your love! To cousin **Tony**, I remember going to your wedding when I was younger. Big bro spoke fondly of you.

Thank you to my cousin **Corey** Lorenzo "Doonbuggy" Berry. We grew up running around granny's house together. I miss the sound of your voice saying, "What up, Rae Rae!" Thank you for allowing me to use your name as inspiration in this piece.

A special thank you to E.A Wright (Writing Warriors) for my book cover and interior images. To Nicole & Liz of Martin Printing, for creating such amazing, branded material for me, for reading my work, and supporting the resistance! ✊

Thank you to my editor, Monica Wesolowska, for helping me make this the best story it could be. Thank you to my copy editor, Reid Tang. And my proofreader, Carmen-Nicole Cox. My favorite author, Toni Morrison, once said, "The good editors make all the difference." I agree.

Thank you, Ms. Pam. You read this story when it was just a seed, and you believed in my work and in me, even then. I am grateful for your continued spiritual guidance from the other side. I miss you.

Thank you to Fisk University, this is my love letter to you. You took in a little wild child from the southside of Chicago and helped me blossom into a beautiful woman without putting out my fire. You taught me how to make it burn brighter. Fisk Forever! ♥♥

Thank you to all Fiskites, past, present, and future. Including, Nikki **Giovanni** (Thug Life), Judith **Jamison**, John **Lewis**, Diane **Nash**, and W.E.B **DuBois,** your legacies live through us. Thank you for all you have done to pave the way for us and the work you've left behind as the blueprint. It is an honor to pay homage to you through this work.

While I was finishing up this book Nikki Giovanni and Judith Jamison both became ancestors. May your spirits continue to ignite us.

A special thank you to Professor Linda T. Wynn, who taught a Womxn in the Civil Rights Movement class where I learned about the significant contributions of womxn like Diane Nash, Ella Baker, Septima P. Clark, Fannie Lou Hamer, and countless others.

Rest in spiritual peace, Dr. Mitchell. Thank you for teaching me about the history of Fisk and preparing me to not take no "Billy-back bullshit" out here in this world.

To the real Dr. Collier: thank you for introducing me to Ms. Zora Neale Hurston.

And to Dr. Quirin, I couldn't have made it through Fisk without you. You were the gentle yet firm hand I needed during that time in my life. I will always love you for seeing me as I was, and as the flower I would blossom into. Thank you for not giving up on me.

Thank you to one of the world's greatest historians, Dr. John Hope Franklin, who Franklin University is affectionately named after in both Rainbow and this book. Fisk Forever! 🖤🖤

Thank you to The Naturals: April MF Hill, Kenneth Gilkes, Deon Robinson, Doran Senat, and Leah Eneas. I know the universe will bring us together to collab on something artistically special one day. I love y'all. Thank you for supporting your sister-in-love.

In loving memory of the beautiful members of Mother **Emanuel** AME Church. Rev. Clementa Pinckney, Cynthia Graham Hurd, Tywanza Sanders, **Myra** Thompson, Rev. **Sharonda** Coleman-Singleton, Rev. **Daniel** L. Simmons, Sr., **Ethel** Lance, Rev. DePayne Middleton-Doctor, and **Susie** Jackson. And to the beautiful souls of **Tamir Rice**, **Eric Garner**, **Michael Brown**, **Trayvon Martin**, **Rita Hester**, and **Matthew Shepherd**. And although C.J Malcolm is a fictional character; we know stories like this one are all too real and true. We will *never* forget. Black Lives Matter. Black Trans Lives Matter. Yesterday, today, and forever.

Thank you to **Marsha "Pay It No Mind" Johnson** for showing us what it looks like to love ourselves and our identities, while paying others no mind!

Thank you to all our Black military veterans who serve our country and come back to the same country that does not serve them in return. (Shame!) Y'all the real MVPs! Although Monica Jacobs & Lorraine Cuttleston are fictional characters, I was inspired to write about this situation by a post I came across about two Black womxn jailed in Kuwait on false charges. Their names are Monique Coverson & Larrissa Joseph. Please look them up. Their story is one that deserves to be known and told.

Thank you to Ms. B. Fanta Malika Grange for seeing me, pouring into me, and making space for me. You have a heart of gold! I am blessed to know you. And thank you to A Seat at the Table Bookstore; you all truly provide a seat in the community for all of us. You will always hold a special place in my heart for being the first bookstore to put my book on your shelf. I appreciate your support!

Rainbow Peeps & Friends, I truly thank and appreciate each one of you! Whether this is your first time reading my work or if you've read Rainbow or my blogs on verdearzu.com, listened to my podcast Verde's Folding Chair, and/or support me on social media, thank you! As an independent author whose mission is to make space in mainstream publication for myself and other Black. Queer. Womxn. Writers. Your support is crucial.

If you've enjoyed Promise Keeper, please spread the word to your family & friends, on social media, your local independent bookstores, and your local library! Hell, if you didn't enjoy it, spread the word anyway! Thank you!

There was a time in America where it was illegal—against the law for Black people to read and write. The punishment could be as costly as death. That time wasn't so long ago. In fact, aren't the powers that be trying to take us back to that time? Our ancestors resisted then as we resist now. And we will resist forever. Every story we tell, every word we write is the resistance!

In the words of Jamie Foxx, "they erase, we replace." We are our ancestors' wildest dreams. And Promise Keeper is officially written in the stars our ancestors once prayed beneath. We are the original storytellers.

Y'all already know…last but certainly not least, thank you to *ME*! In the words of the great philosopher, revolutionary leader, entrepreneur, and more, Nipsey Hussle, "I just didn't quit. I went through every emotion. I went through every emotion trying to pursue what I'm doing." And this is just the beginning. #TheMarathon-Continues 🏁

And to my wife, My Love, my life partner, my best friend, my passionate lover, my support system, My Six! Thank you for believing in this wild, crazy dream of mine. And not just believing in me and my dreams but also investing in me and my dreams. I love you, babe! Your trust and belief in me mean the world! I'm so blessed our spirits found each other in this physical world. Here's to more adventures of Carmen & Verde! Peace. Love. And Rainbows!! ✊🖤& 🌈🌈

Promise Keeper

A Playlist

"Afro" (Freestyle Skit)—Erykah Badu

"All Eyez On Me"—2Pac, Big Syke

"Work"—Charlotte Day Wilson

"That's Alright"—Laura Mvula

"Sunset" (feat. Yuna Zarai)—The Internet, Yuna Zarai

"Cranes in the Sky"—Solange

"Sex Therapy"—Robin Thicke

"Screwed" (feat. Zoë Kravitz)—Janelle Monáe, Zoë Kravitz

"Slow Dance"—John Legend

"Black Parade"—Beyoncé

"Me Against the World"—2Pac, Dramacydal

Epilogue:

"This Lil' Game We Play"—Subway, 702

To learn more about Verde Arzu and support her work, visit www.verdearzu.com. Become a member of our ever-growing Rainbow Peeps & Friends community on:

Instagram: **@the_writer_verde_arzu**

TikTok: **@verde_arzu**

Threads: **@the_writer_verde_arzu**

LinkedIn: **@Verde Arzu**

BlueSky: **@verdearzu.bsky.social**

Fanbase: **@verdearzu**

You can also listen to her podcast, Verde's Folding Chair, a podcast about making space at the table for Black. Womxn. Independent Writers, and marginalized people. Available on all podcast platforms. Season 3: Coming Summer 2025!

Subscribe to Verde's YouTube Channel: The Writer Verde Arzu **[click that subscribe button!]** Be sure to tell a friend and remind them to tell a friend, until we're all connected as Rainbow Peeps & Friends!

Thank you,

The Writer Verde Arzu

www.ingramcontent.com/pod-product-compliance
Lightning Source LLC
Chambersburg PA
CBHW030126010826
48973CB00002B/449